TRAVIS FEEZELL

Home On the Line

To those who have wandered and come home.

Appetizer

JACK

Her call came during the Sunday breakfast rush. The challenge wasn't in the unexpected surprise, but in the timing. It's really the worst moment of the week, worse even than Saturday dinner. Sunday morning has its own rhythm of constancy, a cacophony of sound and orders and smells that never lets up. It's a beast. Usually I try to avoid it but sometimes I'm caught between a rock and sous chef, or in this instance a sous chef who called in and said he couldn't make it. So they called me. That was actually the first call of the day. This one was my second.

Sunday is the brownstone crowd. After the first cup of coffee at home, they grab the Times and then head over. We're the "hey-let's-go-to-our-favorite-breakfast-spot-this-morning-and-hang-out-all-fucking-day-and-annoy-the-shit-out-of-the-servers" kind of place. It's a kumbaya kind of place as well. We get your gays of course, but also your straights, your young couples with first child they're trying to shut the fuck up, the old farts alone in their thoughts, the well-heeled, and generally the folks trying to get a glimpse of New York City life before heading "out" for the day. Mostly it's local. Places like ours get trashed in the Wednesday "Food" section reviews if they get seen at all.

We do comfort and familiarity. We don't do tweezers or nasturtium leaves or some fucked up sea urchin roe in a roasted barley jus. No foams or airs or gelee, no French pastry or Spanish tapas or Vietnamese pho, no scented flavor pearls. We are not an "experience", only sustenance.

"Jack, you got a call on line two!"

I barely heard my name over the din of the breakfast prep in the kitchen. Some have described a restaurant kitchen as a carefully orchestrated symphony, an aesthetic flow of server, prep cook, sauté man, and sous chef. There is a conductor, he – or increasingly she – of the restaurant title, an eponymous finger-pointer gathering up the disciples to make what he – or she – wants. That's fucking bullshit. No kitchen is like that. Kitchens are more like car wrecks with really, really pissed off people yelling at each other with increasing volume and quantity as the time wears on. Get me this, we're out of that, down two of this, where is my fucking spatula.

"Fuck" is a favorite angry kitchen word along with "bitch" and "balls" as in "Get me that fucking spice right now, you little bitch, or I'll shove your balls in your mouth!" And those are the people in the kitchen who might actually be friends. I've seen some folks so angry they flip hot grease at a colleague, not big pools of the stuff, but enough to leave a blister or four. And it's subtle … oh, I'm sorry I didn't see the moisture on that, and you were right there when I put it in oil, and I didn't mean it … "Sorry," they say, in the best sorority voice one can muster.

"Jack, your call is still holding on line two!" That's Pedro, that fucking little bitch. Ok, I know I sound racist but it's not a fucking myth that most of the workers in any New York City restaurant, four-starred or otherwise, are Pedro's and Manny's and Hernandez. They're here – a bit under the table of course and usually undocumented – but working for ten bucks an hour is like finding a gold mine for some. Twelve-hour shifts times that ten bucks plus a little from the tip jar means a decent financial windfall for the day. Plus you're getting some free food along the way. Do that six days a week for a month and you can barely eke out a living in some shithole place out in Bed-Sty, especially if you're putting a dozen people in a two-bedroom apartment. Look, I'm not a racist nor am I an activist and I realize this shit sucks, I'm a humanist and I'm a sous chef. I work at a restaurant, not the fucking United Nations. I need my dishes clean, my knives sharp, and my fucking stock and vegetable prep done just right. Some white dude off the street won't do that for ten bucks an hour under the table, but Pedro will. And he does a goddamn supreme vegetable prep.

"Jack, will you please get the fucking phone? I've got orders backing up!"

That's Jenny, the maître d 'bitch and organizer of all-things- front-of-the-house. She's cool. We slept together a few times and even tried to be a couple for about a month. It sucked and we knew it. I am not settled geographically or emotionally, especially emotionally. At thirty-eight I'm still a pin head that cooks, likes a decent beer, a joint now and then, reads shitty World War II spy novels, thinks Pilates is a fucking waste of brain matter, and still gets geeked out over an unbelievable meal. Oh yeah, porn is for morons. I got over that in my mid-twenties. So maybe I'm not emotionally unformed, I'm just emotionally underdeveloped and emotionally unavailable as I try to figure it all out.

Jenny comes screaming into my being again; she is the train wreck and I guess I have to pay attention.

"GET THE GODDAMN PHONE RIGHT NOW JACK BEFORE I CUT YOUR DICK OFF!"

So I drop what I'm doing. I'm the egg guy today after Herve called and said that something had "suddenly come up!". Yeah right, Marcia Brady. I'm pretty sure Herve is either drunk as fuck or he jilted us for another restaurant. My money is on him showing up tomorrow with his two week's notice. The owner will ask my opinion as the "senior" sous chef and depending on my mood – or how good a meal I find tonight – I'll either tell him to kick Herve's ass to the curb because he's a weak little bitch that thinks he's a lot better than he really is OR I'll say let's keep him because I need my Sundays off and I can't fathom cooking eggs until we find someone new.

"Hey Sammy!" – yes, Mexican guy with a white name, it's a long story – "grab my station. I gotta get this. You're down two egg bennies, another over easy, one hard. Scrambles have been in the warmer for ten minutes but they're starting to look like fried pudding."

Sammy comes over, and the transfer of power has occurred. Smoothly, decently, without a "fuck" or a "bitch" or hot oil. It can surprise you sometimes.

I get over to the phone, cover my other ear, just to make out the voice on the line. "Jack, it's me. Get home now, please. She's gone and I need you."

"Me" is my sister in Oklahoma. "She" is our mother. I tolerate the former, detest the latter, and strangely feel moisture forming in my eyes. It's not from the steamer next to me.

Entree'

1

JILL

When I went in to get Mom for breakfast, she didn't move. I pushed, she dented and returned, kind of like Jello. I shook her, she jiggled, again like Jello. I like Jello. I stared at her and gave her my google eyes, like my totally best magic stare that would make her eyes suddenly pop open. Like those dead bodies in horror movies that suddenly come screaming out of their slumber. I love horror movies!

But Mom didn't do that. She didn't spring to life or emerge from the water or come out of her coma. That would have been so cool!

Mom just laid there. I did that thing I've seen on Gray's Anatomy, felt her wrists all the way around, but really I had no clue. I listened to her chest, more Gray's Anatomy. But all I heard was my ear scratching along her pink nightgown. Silence sort of, but not really. I put my hand under her nostrils. Nothing. But I was confused by nothing. I mean, she wasn't waking up but maybe it was the pills. She'd been taking this little blue pill for the last few years and then last year she suddenly took two each night. And last week I saw her take three. I know because after she tucks me in I sometimes sneak back to her door. I think she knows but doesn't let on. I go look because I get afraid that maybe she's disappeared. Do you ever do that? You know, you go back to make sure the door is locked even though you know you locked it? You take ten steps away from it and then wonder if you did it in the first place? You can see yourself doing it, but you're not sure because maybe it's a dream. So you go back to the door, touch it, push it, make sure it's locked, say "I'm locking the door" then walk away only to maybe do it again … and then maybe again. I once wasted the better part of an hour on the locked-door thingy until my mom came home and just wanted to keep the door open to let in some fresh air. She kind of saved me that day.

So anywhoooo … at this point I think Mom is just in a really deep sleep even though she's like Jello. But I'm hungry and she normally makes breakfast. I wandered into the kitchen and began to rummage through the fridge. A bit of bacon, some leftover Gruyere that Mom got last week, along with the usual stuff like Dijon mustard, sherry vinegar, free range eggs, regular stuff that everyone has. I lop together a puffed-up mix between croque monsieur and Welsh rarebit, basically just some yummy cheese toast. Sooo good! We're out of Jamaican Blue Mountain coffee so I have to grind some bold roast Starbucks I find in the back of the pantry. Not bad. But definitely not the smooth silk of the Jamaican. A decent breakfast I guess, considering what I had to work with.

I had given Mom a list of things I needed a few days ago when she was going to travel down to the City, or maybe it was Tulsa, I can't remember. Both are only about two hours away and both have a Whole Foods Market which is the bomb! I've never been there, but I've seen pictures of it and I've definitely been on their website. I used to buy a lot of ingredients online but it would take too long to get to me and it sucked trying to wait when I most absolutely had to get Jamon Iberico for my charcuterie plate. That's ham, real good ham. It got to me in 5-7 business days and tasted like salty cardboard. Not so good. So now Mom travels to Whole Foods at least once a week and I get things right away. So maybe it's not authentically from Spain, but things from there are real good and I can cook all day, right away, if I want.

But Mom didn't go earlier this week. She said she wasn't feeling "up to it", whatever that means in old-lady speak. It really is old-people language. When I watch reruns of "Murder She Wrote" or "Golden Girls" or "Matlock" there's always someone who's not "up to it" and needs to stay home for a nap. Sometimes it's a cover up because they're the murderer! Sometimes they're the victim and get it while they sleep. But either way, not "up to it" is whole lotta old-people stuff.

After breakfast I went back to check on Mom, four or five times, actually, in a couple minute span. Like I said earlier, she didn't disappear. But she just laid there like Jello on one of those small plates you would get at a cafeteria. I've never been to a cafeteria but I saw this show from Andrew Zimmerman who went to the best cafeterias in the country and I swear every single one of them had Jello on a plate, usually red or green with just a dab of whipped cream on the top. Andrew didn't even eat the Jello, he just pointed it out at each stop like "Oh my God, this is the best fried chicken I've ever had … and look, Jello again!"

I went in to watch TV, my normal routine. The 9am hour is usually reruns like Fantasy Island or Love Boat, you know the short "da plane, da plane!" guy or coked-out Julie, the cruise director who I now know everything about because we got internet. I wrote both of them letters but I didn't get anything back. I love those shows. I think I've seen every single one of them so I know to switch back and forth depending on the story. I mean really, the stories are usually the same and everyone is happy in the end, but my favorites are when the couples decide to get a divorce. I know it's mean and my Bible says I shouldn't be mean, but it's like real, you know?

10am is when I get real serious. Usually it's a rerun of Iron Chef on Food Channel though once I turned it to PBS and saw this cool Scandinavian cooking show. There was this guy who set up his kitchen outside right next to this white house and a stream. It was pristine, I tell you! He cooked up a dish of sautéed reindeer filet with lingonberry sauce. I asked my mom to stop in at IKEA the next week to pick up lingonberries and deer. We settled for a nice filet mignon of cow because it seems IKEA doesn't carry deer.

Iron Chef rocks. My favorite is Bobby Flay but I really like Cat Cora a lot too. Clean and efficient cutting techniques, creative dishes, perfect textures. Well, I don't know if the textures are right, it's just what the judges say. One time they battled each other and I didn't know who to root for. It ended in a tie, the one and only tie on the show. Cat did a French-inspired chicken dish sous vide while Bobby did a real muscular soup-stew thing that was Asian. A little curry paste, lemon grass, noodles, that kind of cool street-food thing, but with panache. I think they call it "elevating the norm" or some stupid label. We still have some dried lemon grass and a can of coconut milk that Mom bought for me after that show. It's getting dusty in the pantry, but you never know.

After Iron Chef comes the bitching hour, or three bitching

hours to be exact.

Rachel Ray, Paula Deen, and Giada DiLaurentis. Bitch, bitch, bitch. I watch because there is nothing else on. I tried some other reruns once. Family Guy, Happy Days, Cheers, My Best Friend's Mother. But when everyone else was laughing, I didn't get it. So I went back to the three bitches.

Rachel makes meals in thirty minutes but it's for morons. You know, "This is an onion, chop it finely, now pour oil in the pan, add the onion, now gently stir it until brown." She's too homey and probably shops every day at the local Piggly Wiggly like my mom's friends, except Rachel knows what an avocado is and tries to teach everybody how to make guacamole. And don't get me started on Paula Deen. Another chef – Anthony Bourdain – called her fat. Everyone was outraged, outraged, I tell you! But I laughed. Actually I wrote him a letter also to say how much I agreed with him. I mean really, how many dishes can you actually do with Duke's mayonnaise? Giada? Big head, big boobs, terrible cooking.

Lunch comes after the three bitches, usually leftovers from the night before. With only the two of us, I make big batches of things that give us leftovers. Mom eats them when she takes her lunch three days a week to her job at the Co-op. She comes back and tells me how Janice loved the pesto or that Jim loved the vegetables and aioli. She asks me once in a while if they can come over for dinner but I'd really rather not.

She also tells me I shouldn't eat so much because I'll get bigger than I already am. I'm not that big I guess. I wear a size large in most things and that seems kinda normal cause Paula Deen's probably wearing an XL or bigger! I don't really wanna look like all those skinnies on TV. Even if I don't look like Paula she seems more normal. I guess I gotta watch what I eat now and then. I don't really get out much and exercise. Actually I don't go out at all and I tried to exercise a while back, sit-ups and yoga and stuff but it was tres boring.

So lunch ends, and my talk shows begin. Dr. Phil all the way through Ellen. I kind of dig Maury especially, just 'cause he's so out there. One time he had a whole group of people who liked to dress up as stuffed animals. There was even a convention they were attending that week with meetings for teddy bears, horses, even those weird stuffed clowns. When Maury asked them why, the guests said, "Why not? It's harmless and helps us escape from the real world." This was a guy who normally serves as a firefighter. Great, now my fires are being fought by stuffed animals. Actually, think about it … how cool would it be for a guy dressed as a stuffed dog to rescue a cat from a tree? I bet it's on YouTube or AFV.

I like Dr. Phil a lot. Ever since he told me what I have that keeps me here, I've been glued to his show. Every Monday through Friday, 4pm, no if's, and's, or but's. I keep thinking that maybe he can tell me a little more about my condition, but so far nothing. Yesterday he had on some people who treat their pets like children and how it was causing issues in the family. One lady had gone so far as to get braces for her wiener dog to cure a nasty gap in his teeth.

So I got through watching Dr. Phil and went to check on Mom again. Still nothing, even after the sixth or seventh time I went in there. Man those blue pills are strong. I wandered into the kitchen to see what was for dinner. Not much, it appeared. With her not feeling "up to it" and not having gone to the store, we were getting down to nothing. But a bit of pasta, some sunflower seeds, garlic, and basil from the windowsill garden make an excellent pesto. Voila! Or bam! Emeril rocks.

By this time it's getting on to 7pm. It's funny because I'm not much of a prime- time television watcher. Too much drama and like I said, I don't get the jokes on the comedies, especially the ones with all the "friend" groups. I don't really have friends so the in-jokes about stinky breath and bad hair or fears of spiders goes straight over my head. I just can't relate. Instead I'll sometimes watch Top Chef – Tom is sooo cool! – or some Gordon Ramsay show – not as cool but pretty funny when he starts yelling at people in the restaurant. But I can't remember ever going out for dinner so those are usually out there. And when TV won't do, I'll get on the internet. I don't do emails or chats but I'll look at food blogs and web pages. It takes up a lot of my time and I get a new idea now and then. And suddenly bedtime arrives and it's the end of another day. I say my prayers, usually the Lord's Prayer and one more about keeping my house safe from kitchen fires, and it's off to la-la land.

When I wake up again, I can already tell it's later than it should be. The light in my window isn't right and I'm downright famished. Why didn't I wake up? I know, it's too silent. Mom would usually be up and she's noisy. Really, that woman is never silent except when she lays in bed like Jello. Usually I'd hear the toilet flush or the door opening while Mom goes outside to check the weather. She grinds the coffee and bangs dishes in the kitchen. But not today. None of that. It's just silence. It's bewildering.

One foot seems to pull me out of bed, then another into her room. But I'm slow … and worried. If Mom isn't there then what will I do for breakfast? We're out of breakfast. I know, I checked last night. Maybe that's where she is, gone to the store after finally waking up. She slipped out quietly I bet, no coffee grinder, just gone so we can stock up. Mom's good like that.

I step into her room. She's still there. But I can tell it's not Jello any more. It's more like bread left out for a day or two. Stiff, hard, pale, ready for bread crumbs or croutons. Bread like that is lifeless. And at that moment, I know. She's gone, dead, no more. And I panic. Not a little bitty panic, but a full-on, fall-down, crumble, can't-move-a-limb, life-numbing panic. Dear God, what am I going to do? I can't go out, but if I stay I'll wither away to nothing. It's not just a rock and a hard place. It's death for me. But do I want my life to linger away slowly? Or do I want to step outside and feel the worst sort of pain that will overwhelm me and kill me instantly?

In my haze, I take one last glance at my mom. I'm filled with hate and anger because she's left me in such an awful lurch. But at that moment I spy the phone next to her stale- bread body. And next to the phone is the "paper". The PAPER! A long time ago Mom had said that if anything happened to her that I was to go to the phone by her bed and call the number on the paper. They would come help. When I asked who it was she said never mind. And that was that. So here I was with a phone and a scrap of paper as my only lifeline. I lurched toward it and there written in tight block letters is the name I dread most. There are two numbers under that. One says "cell", the other says "work". I know the cell number but I've never called him at work.

I dial and someone tells me to wait. I hear screaming, pans banging together, a ruckus really. And when I think I'm forgotten and will just die here with this phone in my hands, a voice comes on the phone.

"It's Jack … speak and hurry the hell up. I've got shit getting cold"

I tell him it's me and that Mom died. And that he needs to come home.

2

JACK

"Jack, are you there?" The voice was whiny and thin, somehow made even more so because I knew it was from halfway across the country and Jill isn't really thin with anything. There was a silence after she asked, almost twenty seconds or more. And if you know silences of that length, then you definitely know how awkward it can be and how the silence turns itself on the persons involved.

"Yeah Jill, I'm here." But I wasn't really. I felt a long way from here–or there, for that matter. "What happened to Mom?"

"I don't know, she just like, didn't wake up yesterday. I mean, I shook her and all, but nothing happened. So I'm hungry and and we've got nothing to eat here."

"Jesus fuck, Jill, you mean Mom is there with you? You haven't called anybody for twenty-four hours and she's just *there*?" The incredulity in my voice was contributing to my rising temper and a rising volume.

"Well, yeah, but who else am I supposed to call?"

"Jill, we worked this out years ago. In case of an emergency you were supposed to call Uncle Ray. He has the spare key and can come over to check on you. He's the guy, not me. Remember?"

"But it wasn't an emergency … until now. And I don't want to talk to Ray. I need you! Not Ray!" Her tone was rising also and it was anxious and scared and full of the unknown. "He's mean and he sometimes rolls his eyes at me plus he smells like stale onions, you know when they sit in the cellar too long and get moldy around–"

"Jill, Mom is dead. DEAD!" I said it so loud that people in the kitchen were looking up from their stations. Conflict always does that. You can't look away from a fight, even if it is private and none of our damn business.

"I know!" She was wailing at this point. Fuck the hunger, fuck the fear, she was into melt down. "Help me!" It was years and years of anguish coming through the phone. Years of what-ifs. What if I don't have food? What if Mom dies? What if I have to go outside? Panic. That's it. Like when the plane is going down and we can't do a damn thing. Some people accept the future. Most of us fucking freak out. Like Jill.

Fifteen more seconds passed. Silence again. Her whimpering on the phone, me trying to sort out a situation that was turning ugly and dangerous all at once. I think Jill could tell I was trying to get a plan together and this seemed to calm her. Either that or she could hear the kitchen at work behind me. How in God's name she could be put at ease with twelve people huddled in a ten by ten space and yelling "down three eggs" or "fire up the broiler" was beyond me.

"Ok, look, I've got to call Ray. Even if you don't like him, he's got the key and can help. I'll tell him to call the mortuary up in town to come get Mom. If they come before he does, you've got to let them in, right? They won't hurt you, they just need to get Mom out of there. Just point out where she is and then you can go back to your room and watch TV. Do you have enough to eat?"

"Yeah, I think so but we're running out of everything."

"If I asked Ray to bring a few things, would that be OK?"

"Yeah, well maybe. Some fruit, some pasta, a little parmesan, and we're out of garlic. I'm thinking Italian for a meal right now."

"Jill, stop it." I said it like I was talking to a misbehaving three year-old. I didn't scream.

Look, I'm volatile as fuck but somehow I knew that yelling was only going to make it worse. "I'll have him bring some basics, OK? Nothing fancy, just enough until I can get there."

"Fine." A simple "fine" but it was as if I had slapped her. Sullen. How could a fucking forty-two year old woman be this way? I knew the answer. A body that aged normally, an emotional capacity that didn't grow after she hit puberty.

I went back to the encouraging route to see if I could draw her out again. "I'll try to be home tonight, but I don't know when the last plane leaves for Wichita or Oklahoma City. Hell, I don't know if they even go there from JFK or Newark, but I'll be back as soon as I can. Tomorrow morning at the latest. We'll sort it out from there. Sound OK?"

"K." More sullen. Jill was still pissed more at the lack of classic Italian tonight rather than her angry brother or dead mother.

"Love you. I gotta go and get on this." The "love" thing was reflexive. Somewhere in there I probably loved my sister out of allegiance, probably the same for my mom.

"K." And she hung up.

I put the phone back on its hook and stood still. Even in the din of the breakfast service, I felt quiet. It was a time when I should have been remembering my mother, if only fleetingly, as she once was. Not the bitch she had become, but who I know she was. We hadn't seen each other in three years and the conversation since that point had been perfunctory at best. No warmth, only a clinical exchange of information we both needed to move on in our own ways. But there was a time when she had been ok, a real mom, one with kindness and joy and energy. No foibles, without any bad characteristics, just Mom, simple and unadorned and lovely.

But my sister was petrified right now. Beneath her sullen "k's" and middle-aged appearance was a scared child who hadn't quite moved on from her adolescent years. She didn't have Mom. I had seen that kind of fear in her twice before, once when she was fifteen, another time in her early twenties. Both times had been scary, real fucking scary. The first was when Mom wanted to take us clothes shopping but Jill wouldn't go. When Mom tried to grab her hand to pull her along and just get moving, Jill freaked, I mean freaked, to the point of clearing the fuck out of her way because she might hurt us. She grabbed a kitchen knife and said she would kill herself before she took a step outside again. She looked my mom in the eye and said in a neutral voice – scarier than anything I have ever heard to this day – that before she killed herself she would take her down as well. It wasn't gory, it wasn't threatening in that kind of fake bravado shit kind of way. It was matter-of-fact, that if Mom made another move to take her outside, she was going to kill her. She meant it. Every word of it. Mom knew it too. In as soothing a voice as she could muster, one filled with equal parts courage and pain, she relented. And just as delicately, she removed the knife from Jill's hand and took her in her arms. Only when she was holding

Jill did I see just the slightest shadow of resentment. It was my first visit with the great human oxymoron. How can you both hate and love someone at the same time?

The other time I saw Jill's panic was when she cut herself while chopping vegetables. By her twenties Jill was pretty much glued to the food shows on TV. No shit, she would often practice by candlelight. I thought it was weird but my interpretation of it then was that she was in some sort of sex-themed reverie with Tyler Florence. Here Tyler, let me make this wonderful roast lamb for you by candlelight while we talk of nonsense. Anyway, she was trying to mince an onion and instead made a delicate mince mess of her pointy ass finger. Did I say mince? I meant slice because she about took that fucker off. Blood and shit went everywhere and her dangly little middle finger – so appropriate I think – sprayed to and fro to the beat of her heart. She screamed, covered it up with a dish towel after a quick rinse, and then went back to go chop some more. Mom said she wanted to take a look at it.When she did and said "that one is gonna need stitches so let's go to the hospital" Jill flipped. It started as "No, Mom, I'm okay," but when Mom kept pushing, it escalated quickly to threats of self-immolation and murder again. Mom backed down quick. I was the one who ended up sewing her finger back on. Yeah, that's right, back on. Not sewn back up, but on. I was in Home Ec and CPR/First Aid that semester so I did a reasonable job. A decent stitch pattern and a decent idea of how to stop blood from escaping a wound will get you halfway to a degree in surgery. Her finger has never been straight since then, but at least it's all in one piece. Funny how we can settle for the least common denominator in the face of our greatest fears. As long as it takes the fear away, we're all good.

I finally slid away from the phone and sidled up to the greeter's station.

She was just coming back from seating an older couple, regulars who I knew ordered their grits and bacon in a certain way. They must have been from the South.

"Hey, where's Franco?" Franco is the general manager of our place, pure Brooklyn with a smidge of Jersey Shore, especially the hair. Even though I'm the sous chef – a second-in-command on the cooking side of things and completely in charge today because the chef gets Sundays off, the bastard – I still answer to somebody.

Authority, man. It sucks.

"He just walked in, counting receipts from yesterday. Surprise, right?"

When I got to his office, Franco was knee deep in receipts and financials. I could tell because of the chaos of paper on his desk. It's odd because you might think in restaurants that it's all about the experience, the ambience, all that front page of the *Times* "Dining" section bullshit. Never further from the truth. It's a business. It's here for the dollars. Pretty simple, really. Restaurants either make money or they don't. If they don't, they fold, gone, to the great restaurant heaven in the sky which I assume is populated by loads of places. Elegant places, dives, themed cateries, places that thought you could actually make food with microscopes, tweezers, and cryogenic stasis machines. *Yeah, I'll have that twig made of frozen Portobello dust. And I'll pay fifty bucks for it.* Yeah, that's who's in restaurant heaven.

"Franco, I need some time off. I gotta get outta here 'cause my mom died and my sister's freaking. I'll give you a call in a couple of days to let you know when I'll be back but it shouldn't be more than a week."

Franco paused over his receipts. Now he's younger than me – he's early thirties–but still assumes an air of authority because of his "general manager" title. Word on the streets was that he had gotten some shitty business degree in management from Rutgers or some other place and then had tried to get his MBA but flunked out the first year. Couldn't pass accounting and couldn't write a paper without "yo" in it. Fucking Jersey.

When I asked him for the time off I could tell he was somewhere between pissed and sympathetic. Well, maybe not sympathetic because he couldn't give a fuck about my mom – he only cared about making money and when your sous chef is out for a week that could cause real problems. So maybe his look was more one of obligation, like he felt he had to at least look sympathetic because that's what you do when someone is having a hard time. I'm sure he learned that in his first management class at Rutgers. More likely he was pissed because of the shitty receipts and his one decent sous chef in the last two years – applause, applause, I'll be here all week! – was taking off for a while. He knew he needed to say something, I mean fuck, the guy in front of him just had his mother pass away. Even Jersey guys from Brooklyn have a heart somewhere beneath their buff muscles and hair gel. But it's a tiny heart at best. So he gave me something more neutral.

"Uh, yeah, isn't home like somewhere in Ohio? That's kind of far." And that was the central question, wasn't it?

"It's Oklahoma. Different 'O' state, a thousand miles away, roughly, from Oklahoma. No cowboys in either one and yes, we have running water."

It was my standard answer about Oklahoma. People in

NYC think the Midwest starts once you cross the Pennsylvania border and move into Ohio. It's where culture ends and a civilization of log fires and well water begins. Ohio gets lumped in with Oklahoma (an "O" state) and Iowa (it sounds the same as Ohio). Indiana and Illinois are interchangeable, but Chicago gets a nod. Big city there, you know. Michigan is sort of in the consciousness but only because Detroit makes cars. It would be just south of Montana for all people know. And then the swath of the Dakotas, Nebraska, Kansas, and Oklahoma sort of disappear. And I guess I'd argue that Oklahoma is more "South" than it is the Midwest or the Plains. I've spent time in Mississippi and Arkansas and Alabama and I'd swear Oklahoma and those states are kinfolk. Oklahoma and other states in that general vicinity – except Texas because it's too fucking big – is no man's land. In the minds of New Yorkers, no one lives there, no one goes there, no one is actually from there. I have this poster in my apartment, an old cover of *The New Yorker*. It's titled "A New Yorker's Map of the United States." The configuration of states is roughly congruent to the shape of the US, but New York City takes up nearly two-thirds of the entire map. Chicago gets a blip and Florida gets a fair shake – it's West Palm of course – and then there's this span of nothingness, no label whatsoever, until you reach California. That's it, the NYC mindset.

"Yeah, Oklahoma, I remember now. How long you planning on being gone? We're struggling here, and I gotta get this right. You're my kitchen guy and the raw materials are knocking us dry. You know, cheese and eggs and veg. We gotta do better."

It was kind of surreal. Here my mom had just died, my sister was freaking and Guido from Jersey was giving me shit about being gone and costs going up. I should have been pissed. But it just wasn't there anymore. I hadn't talked to my mom in ages, my sister was a whack job, and Pauly from the Shore was right. We were hemorrhaging money in this restaurant. Even then, I needed to go home, if only to set it all back to some semblance of order.

"Look, I said I'd be gone for a few days, a week at most. I gotta go, it's my mom. I'll finish this shift then we'll talk costs for the next two weeks. Then I'm out, OK?"

He nodded and went back to looking at his receipts. Real Jersey warmth. I love it.

3

JILL

I waited around for Uncle Ray to show up. It seemed like forever but I think it was only twenty minutes or so after I hung up with Jack. He must have called Ray right away.

"Jill, you there?" Ray kind of has this squealy voice and it really sounded awful as he was banging on the screen door.

I had been sitting in the kitchen pondering my next meal, so it was an easy stroll over to the screen door through the front porch. He looked scared and jittery but trying to seem solid. But he wasn't. He never was. I knew that from way back when.

"Uncle" Ray wasn't really any relation to us at all. He lived a quarter-mile down the dirt road on a forty-acre quarter spread. He owned three other quarters and farmed wheat each year like every other farmer in our patch of Oklahoma. God, what a rube! Incidentally, I love that word rube. I picked it up off an old Love Boat episode where Doc called Gopher that after some serious hijinks.

Anyways, I'd known Ray all my life. As the story was told to me, Ray was a good friend of my daddy's. His home had been in his family for ages, kind of like our house. I guess it got passed down from dad to son and so on and so on since the days of the Oklahoma land rush whatever that was. I think I learned about in school but that was like in third grade, ages ago.

In our family it was a little different. Daddy had come to work on our farm one summer; Granddaddy had an extra big harvest that year so he needed some extra help. Dad was a wanderer who traveled on the trains so he showed up in our patch of Oklahoma, coming from California or somewhere else out there, and looking for a few days of work. He worked the fields with Ray and they became best buds. But Daddy also fell in love with the farmer's daughter. That would be my mom. Granddaddy didn't like it but he had no choice. My grandmother who I never knew had died a few years before and my mom was his only child, his only girl. And of course, who could do the cooking and the cleaning if she was going to run off with a wandering farm worker? No one, silly! So my granddaddy let them get married. He ended up passing away the next year and suddenly my daddy and mommy had a farm all to themselves. And my daddy had a best friend down the road. He and Ray were real good friends. And since Mom had no siblings and neither did Daddy, he became "Uncle" Ray.

Daddy died when I was twelve and had asked Ray to "take care" of us. I'm not sure what taking care means, but as far as I can tell it meant he farmed our land. I remember going over to Ray's place a few times when I was young. It was pretty cool as a kid. Mom would let me walk there on my own. I especially remember walking there in the summer. I'd set off down the dirt road and a quarter-mile seemed like forever.

The road would get cloudy where I kicked up dirt and I would meander into the shelter belt of trees to pick up a rotting gourd from the vines that created a forest of mystery. Super cool! I would take those old smelly gourds and throw them against the trees, playing war against any Commie bastards that might come my way. Or I might tear up bits of gourd and drop them on my way to Ray's, pretending I was going to the Wicked Witch's house and needed to trace my escape. Oh my God my hands would stink so bad when I did that. Ray would make me wash them three times - really, three times! - before he would let me in the house. And I still smelled like a fart. Well, green Palmolive dish soap, mixed with a fart.

Uncle Ray had this great garden next to his house. Even if he was a rube at farming wheat, that man could grow a garden. It was huge, like taking up half of his front yard which must have been an acre or two on its own. I thought it was so cool to wander in there and see the beans and the eggplants and the corn and the tomatoes. My favorites were the okra and especially the squash. There would be these two little leaves in a mound of soil, but every few days when I would visit, they would seem to expand like a balloon until they were these enormous plants I couldn't get my arms around. And then these pretty flowers would appear, open in the morning, then closing up during the heat of the day. I was in shock when Mario Batali told me I could eat those blossoms and fill them with cheese and fry them. God, those were good. I made them like, seven straight days after that show until Ray wouldn't bring me any more. He said he wanted some squash too.

Ray also had a bunch of abandoned cars in the grove of trees behind the garden. God knows how they got there. Well, obviously someone had to put them there. But there were like five or six cars, lined up almost like a driveway. They were all kind of weird shaped things, like an elephant that got fat. I mean, an elephant is already big and all, but can you imagine a fat, like really huge, elephant? These cars were like that, rounded and bloated and sticking out in places where they shouldn't have. My brother told me once that these were "fins" and they were kind of cool back in the day. Jack was always a car guy. Me, I was the food gal.

There was this one car. My brother saw it later and said it was a 1952 DeSoto. It seemed huge to me, bigger than anything I had ever been in. At first I crawled through open windows (Who leaves abandoned car windows open, I ask?) but later I was able to open the door and get in like a regular person. It always smelled like those rotting gourds, sans Palmolive but somehow that didn't bother me. The interior was this white plastic kind of stuff, a little bit shiny, but also covered in Oklahoma dust that had gotten through the window. I would sit in there and drive, sometimes imagining I was on my way down Route 66 all the way to California – well, it goes through St. Louis, down to Missouri, Oklahoma City. It's oh so easy, you'll see Amarillo, Gallup, New Mexico, Flagstaff, Arizona, don't forget Winona, Kingman, Barstow, San Bernadino – all the way to the Pacific Ocean. Sometimes, I'd go the other direction and drive all the way to Maine, maybe have a lobster roll or two. I would even play house in that car, it was so big. There was a living room, the dining room, and the back seat was definitely the bedroom. I'd sneak back there after a while and sometimes even take a nap. I miss that car. I wonder if it's still there.

I let Ray in because I wasn't sure what else I was supposed to do. Ray is kind of pudgy now; he wasn't that way when I was a kid. He had that skinny farmer look then, a little wrinkled mixed with being old, like he'd been fighting the dirt and the wind all day. But now he just looked pudgy. It was either a sign that he'd given up on farming, just kind of half-assin' it in his air conditioned tractor and combine, or that he had gotten old and fat like most people do. I mean, I've seen Jack LaLane on TV with his amazing vita- mix and that old man is ripped. But most old people seem to get pulled down, their skin and their boobs and their slouched over shoulders, and even their personalities. That was Ray, pulled down by his many years on earth.

He took off his grimy green Monsanto hat and fell across the doorway.

"You OK?" he asked. It was a gravelly voice, dust mixed with two packs a day of unfiltered Marlboros. Oklahoma farmers don't exactly adhere to the Surgeon General's warnings.

"Yeah, I guess. I'm kind of hungry, but I'll get by."

"Where is she?" he queried as he took a few steps away from me, hastening himself closer to Mom's room.

"Dad, slow down!"

That was Beth, Ray's daughter from a first marriage. After Ray graduated from high school, he left to hang out in Norman. Not to go to college–I think he just needed to get away from the farm. At least that's how my mom described it.

So anyway, as Mom tells it, Ray went off to Norman and got a job as a machinist at the physical plant on campus. After about a year there, he hooked up with some chick in a bar, some heiress from Pittsburgh or Buffalo or somewhere. They hung out, he knocked her up, they had a daughter, tried marriage for a year or two, but it didn't work out. She took the daughter - Beth - back to Mummy and Duddy. Duddy cut off the trust fund and the living allowance and Beth's mom just couldn't make do on a machinist's salary. So she left. OK, cliché I know, but one day she's there, the next she's gone with only a note left behind that says, "I love you, but this will never work out. We can still be friends and Beth can visit." Alright, I made the note part up but that's how I imagined it to be. It's always like that on Lifetime shows.

Beth would come back every couple of years to visit so that's how I knew her.

Well, I wouldn't really say I knew her because she was about my brother's age, but sometimes she would walk over on the dusty road to play with Jack and I'd see her then. I remember we talked a couple of times and seemed to hit it off, but really, what do you say to a ten-year old when you're fifteen? It ain't all Barbies and Kens anymore.

"Dad, slow down!" Beth's voice was angrier the second time. But Ray just kept making his way back to Mom's bedroom where, frankly, she was starting to stink. I wanted to say to him–

"Hey Jill … you OK?"

It was the first time she had spoken to me in maybe twenty-five years. Really, the last time I had seen her was when she was seventeen, and she was some weird mix of sophistication and dork, East-Coast-preppy-meets-Oklahoma-Hillbilly, a blossoming flower with no boobs yet and really, really awkward. Who am I to talk? But then I guess she got tired of Oklahoma visits, Ray, of all of this. I heard she went off to some preppy college too, Swarthmore or Haverford-by-the-Bryn Mawr or something or other. My mom told me about it when I saw it on Ray's t-shirt. And I rarely thought of her, even though Ray would sometimes be over and tell us he got a letter from Beth and that she was in Europe or in California or helping some orphan in Guatemala. Whatever.

But now she was older and real pretty. Her hair used to be all pushed back, but now it was shimmering. No really, it was like glowing, I swear. It was auburn, which I totally love and about shoulder height and pulled back to make her face stand out.

And that face was a doozy. She looked *smooth*. That's it, smooth. Especially next to Ray who looked like someone had taken sandpaper–the real heavy grit–to his face over and over, leaving valleys and scars and pits. Beth had skin that was like silk, perfectly smooth. She was slim, not skinny. Skinny stinks. She was perfect, like those anchors on TV news. Not too this, not too that, but a whole lotta presence, like she's-got-it-together presence. And the jeans and the blouse - cream with a hint of rose - were to die for.

"Yeah, I'm OK, a little hungry and kinda bored."

"Look, well, we'll get your mom taken care of and then maybe you can tell me what you need at the store?"

At that moment Ray came barreling back into the kitchen. He was crying, not the sobbing kind of crying, but just real sad, eyes watered over, and some sniffles to back it up.

"Jill, honey, I know you knew …" - sniff, sniff - "I, I know your mom's dead, but she …" - sniff, wipe the eyes - " … she died real peaceful I think. I know she'd had some heart problems lately, but I think …" - sniff, pause, double sniff, pause - "that her heart just kind of gave out. I'm glad you were here so she wasn't alone."

And for whatever reason, that's when it hit me. I was alone and Mom was dead. It wasn't my hunger anymore and it wasn't about TV. It was about me being by myself, alone, and without the one person who took care of me. A tiny anxiety started to build in me then and it emerged as humming.

"UmmmmMMMMMMMMMM…"

"Jill, honey, it's OK. We'll be here. We'll take care of you. We'll …" Ray's voice faded away. He might have kept talking but I really don't know. I lay down on the floor right there in the kitchen. My face was turned to the refrigerator and I vaguely remember seeing all the dust fluttering on the ventilator grill. And I just kept humming, afraid to move or do anything but see the dust bunnies flicker in the breeze of the frig.

"Jill? Jill?" This was Beth. Somehow she knew. She got down right next to me and began to stroke my hair. She didn't say anything, but she was there, even if I had disappeared completely.

4

JACK

I left the restaurant around 2pm after working out the supply costs with Franco.

He was thrilled because we were able to find around two hundred a week in savings. So maybe we'd cut out the side of asparagus in the eggs benedict and replace it with a grilled tomato quarter, but hey, it still had the eggs and sauce, right? Keep the price the same but eliminate some expensive puzzle piece. It was a strategy as old as fucking time in the restaurant game.

While Franco and I were working, I was able to get onto a computer and book a flight. There was a 6pm flight from JFK to Chicago that got me in around 830pm. I had a choice then. I could either do the morning flight to Wichita, which meant a layover near O'Hare, or more likely, sleeping in the airport on some godawful corporate carpet with stains from fuck-knows-what. I'd done that when I went to Eugene in my early twenties, slept in seats on some moving contraption in the middle of the night. Or even better, some desecrated downtown train or bus station with the lowlife of the universe all around. Seemed like a great idea then, real independent and very much a part of my "trekker identity" at the time as I was trying to find myself. What I really found out later was that those lowlife people were hella good and I was a complete idiot, But really, the seats still sucked.

I was pretty wired and could feel the double burdens of my mom's death and my sister's condition setting upon like a great big fucking fog. Nope, crashing in an airport sounded like shit. Instead, I opted for the 10pm flight from Chicago to Kansas City. It would be a four-hour drive over to the farm, but maybe it would do me some good. That would get me to the farm sometime in the middle of the night. I didn't know what to envision when I got there, but somehow, arriving in the cover of darkness made me feel like I could just step onto the scene covertly, maybe survey my surroundings and get my bearings before my sister would crash it all. It had been a while since I'd returned and I needed to reacquaint myself with the place before reacquainting myself with her.

From work I got on the train and made my way back home – well, what serves as a home. Like most cooks and chefs in NYC – those without a TV show or a cookware line – I wanted to gravitate towards two places: Chelsea or Brooklyn. Both have decent rent control, which is nice, and both have amazing food scenes. It used to be experimental or ethnic, sometimes both, up until about five years ago when the tide turned and the foam-and-freeze-dried crowd left. What remained were the authentic places, real Pakistani food run by real Pakistanis and not some fucking CIA (Culinary Institute of America, not spies) douchebag who's into Pakistani this week and essence of some spritzy little sea urchin nothing for his *plat du jour*. What was left in these places were small and intimate gathering spots, some ten seats, others thirty, but all with the soul of a community. They were run by chefs interested in ingredients and taste but mostly interested in pleasing a crowd through their own love of food. It was visceral and heady and sensory, things like meatloaf with caramelized onions and homemade ketchup or a wrap or tortilla with perfectly cooked meat and brined veggies. It was mom's Sunday best, her beautiful church- loving frock, but underneath was a pair of sexy knickers that brought dad to orgasm. I'm telling you that shit was good.

I lived in Brooklyn for a while but those fuckers in the *New York Times* "Food Section" caught onto our scene and began to announce it to the world. I counted once that they had eight straight weeks of reviews of Brooklyn and Williamsburg restaurants. Jesus, why don't you just put out a sign that says, "Morons of the world unite and come to Brooklyn for good eats!". And so our scene became their scene. You couldn't get a seat in those places anymore, even late at night. And the cash flows seemed to change the place itself. The tables and chairs went from Target chic to high end designer shit–nice, but so faux-gritty-restaurant I could puke. The lighting went from cheap- ass lamps to wall sconces covered with sheer linens in purple and pink. And of course, prices went up as well. I don't need mood lighting for thirty bucks a plate. I want to see my food and eat the shit out of it and not feel like my wallet has been skeeved off me.

You can see where this is going. I got the fuck out of Brooklyn and ran to Chelsea. It was weird how it all happened. I knew I had wanted to leave for a while and had concocted a plan to go with the other chefs from work who were feeling the same thing. But instead, those two–a boy and a girl–had boy-meets-girl/girl-meets-boy feelings and fell in love, got engaged, and then moved off to Madrid to work in a kitchen together. All in the space of about a month. So what had been my plan to find a place with them was now me riding solo. And contrary to what most would believe, you just can't live solo on a chef's salary in New York unless you want to exist in a space the size of a closet. I was reading one of the free street rags on my day off. Quintessential NYC and in my best Carrie Bradshaw voice I describe it thusly... *"There I was in a coffee shop reading my newspaper and digesting the sine qua non of the City, sipping a cappuccino and wondering, will I ever find a home?"* Pretentious really, but the truth. Really. I was having a cup of coffee in a Times Square corner deli and reading a leftover paper some previous customer had left on the stool next to me. NYC has a great tradition for funky newspapers. One for the homeless, one about the homeless, one written by the homeless, one for the gay scene, one for the arts, one for the gay homeless artists written by people who want to be artists and were formerly homeless. Anyway, I was thumbing through this thing and reading the want-ads.

"CROSS-DRESSING MALE ACTOR SEEKS STRAIGHT ROOM-MATE TO SHARE A TWO-BED FLAT IN CHELSEA. ONLY SERIOUS INQUIRIES ALLOWED."

That's it. That's all there was. No number, no contact info, just the seeking part. Well, amateur sleuth that I am, I inquired. I called the paper and, after a five-minute wait, got the classifieds editor.

"You're only the second person to ask about this. The guy was really clear that I was only to give out the number if people called me. Hey, for an extra five hundred in my pocket, why the fuck not?"

He gave me the number which I called immediately. And thus was born my long and continually strange trip with Derek, my cross-dressing roommate, he of the burlesque cabaret on 35th, he of the current relationship to Angela, he that is perhaps my best friend ever.

Derek Goldberg is the progeny of academia. His parents come from a long line of Jewish intellectuals. Dad is a professor of sociology and one of the leading authorities on queer studies. Mom is a religious studies prof and Far East religions turn her on. Upon completion of the doctoral degrees both needed jobs and so decided to become dual-track applicants, they of two jobs but one salary. They landed at Grinnell College, one of the hippest outposts in Iowa. Grinnell is in the middle of fuck-all and there is no synagogue to be found, but it did offer colleagues from Harvard and Berkeley, students from East Coast prep schools, decent research money, and ultimately a second tenure-track job for them when push came to shove. Six years later–of course after tenure which had been granted to both–Derek was born.

Iowa is not known for producing heterosexual cross-dressers, generally–look to Nevada or California for that kind of thing– but Derek was different and accepted as such. When you grow up in a home where you can talk about the politics of "the other" over a nice Sunday casserole, it's bound to rub off. Derek told me it began as a kind of innocent gender-bending thing when he was seven or eight, you know, let's play dress up with the kids on the block. But one time it was just him and another boy so one of them was forced to play mommy in this episode of *Midwestern Living*. *Voila!* Derek was in women's clothes. And he loved the shit out of it. He kept it in check through high school, literally keeping it in the "closet", but he told me later his mom confessed she knew what he was doing when he was thirteen. From that time on, even though she never let him know, she'd drop in a new pair of shoes or a dress or some fantastic blouse just for Derek. She never wore them but imagined he would. When she saw them a bit ruffled or out of place in her closet, she felt like a great parent. And she was.

Derek went off to school in the East (shouldn't we all?) at Haverford College because at that point Philadelphia was cool and the whole Quaker thing about living in peace and shit appealed to him. He joined all the liberal causes, became a theatre major, did improv in the student center on open mic nights, and still kept cross dressing to the nines. By this time he had told his parents and frankly they didn't care at all. "An edge is good," proclaimed his dad. "Your edge just happens to include Donna Karan." He tried being gay for six months. I asked him once what "trying" meant. For him it was two partners, one a freshman he had met through the theatre, the other a one-night rebound fuck he had when that freshman said he wanted to "just be friends." Derek knew at that point it was all just an experiment and that the chemicals had all exploded. No more chemicals, no more experiment, no more gay Derek. No matter how much he adored Chanel and matching tops and bottoms with just the right earrings, he knew he was straight.

But the problems of where to go and what to do as a cross-dressing heterosexual theatre major eluded him for a while after college. He worked in Philly as a financial trader but that crowd was too tight and so were the suits that were required every day in the office. From there it was on to a high-end shoe store as a manager and buyer but lo and behold a little bit of Iowa came out of him. As he described it, "Those pretentious motherfuckers wouldn't know the taste of manure if I shoveled cow shit in their mouths. They'll never know shoes like I do!" So that ended after a year.

He wandered up to New York hoping to just chill a bit but

instead he found nirvana. We all know that NYC never sleeps, but what people don't know about the City is that it's an all-you-can-eat buffet of every imaginable social form and deviant flavor.

You got a thing for naked fat broads, there's a strip club for that, doing quite well I'm told, and the ladies make bank. You like Persian porn films? Yep, that too. For a straight guy into dress-up and drag as a woman it was like finding sesame chicken at a Chinese buffet. It's everywhere if you know where to look. And even better, you know the right places to go.

Derek is my best friend, my one true male friend, my confidante. Perhaps my only real friend, period. I tell him everything and he does the same with me as far as I know. I buy him boas for birthdays, he gets me a kick-ass microplane. It works.

I walked into our place. Derek had on a mini skirt and heels but no make up...yet. He was headed out for drinks with the boys and girls, or boys-as-girls. This was his basic Sunday get-up.

"Hey man, what's up? Any more crap from your boss?"

"My mom died."

Simple and to the point. Derek appreciated that. Who needed a paragraph when three words will do.

"Man, I'm sorry. What can I do?"

I'd noticed about six months ago that Derek peppered his language with words like "dude" and "man" and "guy". At first I laughed and pointed it out to him, a walking oxymoron of runway chic and surfer dude patois. He laughed too and even tried to be self-aware and stop the language, but he ended up sounding like a TOEFL tape, you know, teaching English as a foreign language to some guy from Mongolia that's never heard it. "Hello. How are you today? I am fine. Would you care to attend the cinema?"

"Nothing right now. I gotta get going. Flight's booked for KC this evening. My sister's kind of freaking right now."

"Dude, is she OK? I mean like, I'll call her if you need. I talked to her last week and she seemed fine."

As odd as it may seem, and shit with Derek is always odd, he and my sister were pretty tight. Sometimes my sister called when she was bored or when Mom had gone to get things in Oklahoma City. She didn't have anyone to talk to and the food shows and *Love Boat* never talked back. If I was in the right mood, about every six months to a year, I would answer my cell (I never answered at the restaurant). After Jill wore me out, I would turn it over to Derek. And they clicked. She would just call him sometimes. He would ask her what she was doing and she'd prattle on about food and cooking and Mom. But she also asked him…how are you? And no-filter Derek would respond with "Well, I've got this show tonight and my panties, the lacy ones with the roses, are all in a bunch and my skirt needs ironing." Too funny. My wacked-out agoraphobic sister and my cross-dressing roommate became pals. It wasn't some pity party friendship, like oh your sister needs a friend because she is cooped up in the house and has none.

Instead, this was real friendship, *I miss you, good to talk to you, letters and emails.* And they had never met in person, not once. My sister of course couldn't go out. And Derek, well, he refused to venture back to the Midwest, a geographical agoraphobe in his own right.

"Nah, I think she's OK," pausing for a second to really wonder if she was. "Uncle Ray is heading over there to check. I think my mom's still in her bed."

"Dude, that's a little freaky. Dead bodies in beds are not cool."

Silence then as both of us thought about a real dead person in her bed. "Yeah, I guess." It was all I could muster.

"Really man, you OK?" Derek stepped a little closer as he said it.

"Kind of numb, I think. My mom's dead and I really don't know what to feel. I mean she's my mom. But I stopped liking her in high school. I never really wanted to start again with her. She tried and I resisted. When the things you're pissed off at are no longer there, should you still be mad?"

I didn't really feel loss. I suppose that something was there and it wasn't anger or sadness or frustration or anxiety.

"Dude, what you're feeling is empty. That's a feeling all its own. Like in the absence of feeling pissed off there's this hole that's not filled with anything anymore. You'll have to fill it up again."

Derek the fucking philosopher. This is why I loved him. He got me and he got it, whatever IT was supposed to be about the universe.

"So how do I fill it up?" I queried.

"I don't know man. Just go there and figure it out."

5

JILL

I woke up in my bed. I don't know how I got there but it was starting to get dark. Last thing I remember I'd been on the floor. And there was that damn silence again–except for a page turning next to me. I glanced over and saw Beth reading my mom's *Home and Garden*, the August issue that talked about canning and pickling. Why was it every August issue had to talk about canning and pickling? Same with *Good Housekeeping* and *Midwest Living* and *Oklahoma Monthly*. My mom would get all of those. And I got a little sad when I thought of her then.

"Hey there!" Beth had noticed me glancing over at her. Her voice wasn't sickly sweet, more a recognition of me in bed and Mom in the ground.

"What time is it?" I asked hesitantly.

"About 7:30. You've been out for a while. Do you remember when we came over this morning?"

"Yeah, I remember. Didn't I, like, conk out on the floor or something?"

"Yep, we got you settled and then got you up here. You've been out a while. Almost eight hours."

"Eight hours? Oh my God, I'm famished! Can I get something to eat?"

"Sure…but don't you want to talk first, you know, about your mom?" Beth was hesitant, but I could tell she was a little curious too, sort of probing to check if I was OK.

"We can talk some but I don't know what to say. I'm hungry. Do you know how to make an omelet? Cause that sounds good. Wait, we don't have any eggs. How about–"

"I went to the store while you were out. Ray stayed here but I was able to get some things. I went through your fridge. Is that OK?"

"More than OK!" At least in all of this I wouldn't starve. "How about this…" She paused, seeming to try and work it all out. "I'll go make you an omelet, but let's talk when I get back. Do you need anything else?"

"Nope. Just remember to swirl the pat of butter and a low heat is crucial with eggs. Are they free range?"

"No, not free range, just IGA specials. But I get the butter and low heat. I dated a chef once. He turned out to be an asshole, but he taught me some things around a stove. I'll be OK." And she wandered out my bedroom.

She was gone about ten minutes but came back in with a tray of food, one of the bedroom trays with the two legs that go over you when you lay down. On top was a pretty good looking omelet, fluffy, but just a bit burned at the edges. You can always tell an amateur. She had also done a little glass of orange juice and even tossed a few grapes on the side. Altogether quite homey, if I do say so. I hadn't had a plain grape in years. I mean they go great in a chicken and grape roast with balsamic vinegar or in a blue cheese chicken salad, but plain grapes?

"How are you doing?" This was as I was taking my first bite.

Not so cool. But I guess I had been prepping for this question in the ten minutes Beth had been gone. I was doing just fine.

"Fine," I said as I stuffed another bite in my mouth. Even with the burned edges, this was quite good.

"You sure?"

"Yeah." And that seemed to be that. I glanced over at Beth and she had a real pensive look on her face, like she wanted to say more, but was trying to figure out how to do it. So I cut her off at the pass.

"Hey Beth, this is pretty good. Where'd you say you learned how to do this?"

Beth paused like she knew I had turned the tables, but she began to speak in a soft voice. Maybe she was uncomfortable with this whole breakfast-in-bed thing.

"I dated this chef ten years ago. It was in Pittsburgh while I was in graduate school. He worked at an Asian fusion place that was popular at the time, right around the corner from Carnegie Mellon."

That was pretty cool. I'd seen a great restaurants show once that went to Pittsburgh and it showcased this Polish place there. I never really cooked Polish because it looked like a bunch of sauerkraut and overdone meat. Blecch!

"He'd be late at work some nights and would come home at one or two in the morning. I'd be up reading Hegel or Kierkegaard anyway so when he'd finally arrive home, we'd have a little dinner or a late night snack or something. At first he would whip us up something quick so eggs and omelets were often our meal of choice. After watching him for so long, I got the nerve up to try it myself and surprise him. It was awful."

"Burned?"

"No, not burned as much as hard. You know when you cook

eggs too fast?"

"I totally know!" I was like, freaking out because here was someone who knew what I was talking about. Mom never talked food with me even when I tried. She just liked it. Well, most of the time she liked it.

"I remember he took some and sort of chewed it around in his mouth and said, 'Honey, if you want to know how to do this I'll show you, because this is terrible.' I didn't remember his exact words because it was the first time someone had criticized me and I didn't feel bad. The food was awful, but he was willing to help. So I made lots of omelets after that. Sorry yours is off. It's been a while."

"What happened with him?" We were in Love Boat waters.

"He left Pittsburgh. We were together for a long time and started to talk about family and marriage and all those things. But he got a call from a buddy who was just opening up a place in London and wanted my guy to come work for him. He assumed I would come with him."

"Did you go with him?" Total lost love...then reuniting! Oh my God, this was better than any TV show!

"No." She took a while to talk again. Totally out of a movie, cause there seemed to be a memory flickering there. Or maybe regret.

"No, I stayed back. I told him I needed to finish my dissertation and I really couldn't do that in London. I also had two sections of an intro course I was teaching and that was important. But you know what? It wasn't that. I've never told anyone this before, but it wasn't that at all. I was scared. London wasn't my home and I was scared about living. I figured we'd be in London for a year or two and then on to Paris and another restaurant and then off to Brussels or Milan or Madrid."

"OH MY GOD THAT SOUNDS SO COOL!" I couldn't contain myself because I'd seen all those places on TV!

"Maybe. Maybe." She was pausing again. "I guess I just didn't want to go from place to place, never knowing where we'd be and who I would become."

"So what happened?" I totally needed the reunification scene now. Maybe they met up on a cruise and he opened up a restaurant back in Pittsburgh just to be with her.

"Nothing really happened. We said we'd talk and visit and do the holiday thing together, typical crap. But we talked less, didn't visit much, and I was too busy writing to go to London. Can you imagine? Too busy writing about that pissant Kant to go see this guy in London?" She paused again. Sheesh, why so much drama? I think she was trying to collect herself because she seemed to be getting angry. But what came out next was ultra-calm.

"We just stopped. No calls, no letters, nothing. We haven't spoken in like seven years."

That's it? I don't say this out loud, but really, that's it? No happy ending? No getting back together? This wasn't *Love Boat*. It wasn't even *Fantasy Island*. This stinks!

There was more silence for a few moments. I think she was lost in memory. I was just lost. How could she do that? London? Paris? *A man?*

"So what are you doing now?"

"I teach philosophy at Marietta College."

"What, where?" I was confused. She cooked omelets, almost married a chef, almost lived in Europe and now she did what, where?

"That's what I was doing in Pittsburgh, getting my doctorate."

"What's a doctorate?"

"Well, it's a graduate degree. It's a…after high school you go to college, right? Usually you go for four years and then leave to go work. Well I went for four years and then decided to go another seven years. After I was done and wrote this really big book, they gave me something called a doctorate. So my official title is Dr. Beth Schwarzer, Ph.D."

"You're a doctor?" My question was one of awe and anxiety. I didn't really like doctors much–well, except for Dr. Phil. Too many doctors had tried to talk to me over the years and most were just pushy. This one woman was kind of nice though. She talked to me for about six months when I was twenty. But it didn't last. She went away after that. My mom was pretty bummed too.

"Yep, I'm a doctor, but not the kind with needles and a stethoscope. I'm a doctor who talks about words and ideas."

"And you can make omelets!"

"I can make omelets!"

We were both smiling now. I had finished my breakfast meal and we were getting on to bedtime. I was tired even though I had slept eight hours. But I wanted to keep talking. It made me feel better.

"If you teach at Mary Something-or-other, why are you here?"

"It's Marietta. In Ohio. It's kind of a cool place, small town, right next to a river. We have a pretty good baseball team at the college, not so good in football. Have you ever been to Ohi–" She stopped right there because she knew damn well I hadn't been anywhere. "Oh, I'm sorry. Uhm, I'm back because I'm on sabbatical for the year. Sabbatical is like a year when you don't have to teach and you can write and recharge and kind of do what you really want."

"And you get paid? And can go anywhere?"

"Yeah, I get paid!" She said it kind of unexpectedly, like she hadn't thought about it that way before.

"So why are you here, like in Oklahoma?"

"Good question. I haven't seen Dad–Ray–in a while. And I needed a break from Ohio. It's cool and all, but I've felt restless lately, like it's not quite my place to be right now. Does that make sense?"

"Not really. I mean, I'd like to go someplace. I know I really can't, so I just end up staying here and I kind of like it."

She tried again. "It's like you live in the place but you don't feel a connection? Does that make sense? I mean, I have a house and friends and all but..."

"Do you have a boyfriend?" I blurted it out. We were in talk show territory here and I just knew that there was another boyfriend somewhere in here besides the chef.

"Nope, no boyfriend. I dated this chemistry prof for a while. He was older, nice, but kind of square, you know? He saw the world too precisely. We philosophers prefer the world a little messier, like we're not quite sure what's going on. We don't want to measure anything, just ponder it." She smiled then, like she was laughing at her own joke.

"Like a chef who cooks from feel, right?" I was sure I was on to something now. "I noticed that on TV some chefs don't measure anything. They just feel it. I never really understood that until I tried. A bit of this, a touch of that, but somehow I knew how it all fit together even if it wasn't perfect."

"Yeah, kinda like that." Beth was smiling again.

"So how long are you here for?"

"I don't know. I'm not really on a schedule. I need to be back teaching in September so I've got a few months to kill. But I don't know if I'll stay or go. I'm just in a 'being' mode right now and it feels pretty good. And speaking of going, I should probably be off so you can get to bed. I feel like I've talked your ear off. Are you sure you're OK? Do you want to talk about your mom?"

I hesitated because I was starting to feel like I could talk to Beth. But I just didn't know how yet. And I wasn't sure what I wanted to say.

"Nope, not now. Maybe later. But can I ask you something?

"Sure, go ahead."

"Will you stay the night?"

She looked a little shocked, so I chimed in real quick.

"Look, you don't have to and I know we only just talked and aren't like real friends but…I've never slept alone in this house. Ever."

She looked at me funny then took a step closer to the bed where I was still lying.

"Honey, I'd be happy to. I'll grab your plates, come back to check on you and then I'll sleep on the couch. Sound OK?"

It did.

I checked on her six or seven times that night. She watched TV for a while but by the last time I checked, she was asleep.

6

JACK

It never fucking fails that when you really truly need to be somewhere, something is always late. It's like the fucking disclaimer of the universe:

> *Being on time may not happen as expected. Side effects may include shitheads who forget or dumbasses who may go through life with their eyes blinded or their thumbs up their asses. We are not responsible for anything at any time when you really need it.*
> *Love,*
> *The Universe*

So I got into Chicago just fine but the 10pm flight to Kansas City had "mechanical problems". We got on, got settled, and then the cheery voice of the captain comes on.

"Hi folks! I've got a little fuel pump light that keeps coming on. I think it's nothing but we're going to have it checked out before we get started. It should take just a few minutes and then we'll be on our way. We've got someone coming over from maintenance right now."

Cheery motherfucker speaks such bullshit. Who the hell works maintenance on a Sunday night in May. No-fucking-one! So they probably call some schmuck over in Skokie who is just about to get in bed, maybe even get some action with his wife, and then takes about as much time as he fucking can to fix our "little problem".

We got out of Chicago at midnight and finally made our way to the gate at KC around 1:30 in the morning. By this time, I am both pissed and exhausted and in no fucking mood to have anything more go wrong. I wound my way down to the car rental center hoping, just a mere smidgen of hope, that someone might still be there. No luck at all. All the lights were dim and I'm sure I'm staying all night until the counters re-open at 7am.

But maybe the universe was smiling at me like it had fucked with me enough. There's the saying that God only gives us as much as we can handle and maybe Allah- be-blessed-Buddha said it was time. As I was sitting there scoping out my sleeping quarters and the comfiest seats around, I spied a light on under one of the back office doors at Avis. Who knows what compelled me but I marched over and leapt over the counter and walked in. In front of me was a young black man, maybe twenty-two or twenty-three. Fresh faced, but a little weary, heavy, not quite fat, but looking like the weight of the world, Avis and otherwise, had been pushing him down. If you've spent any time living in any big city you know exactly the type. Maybe I expected him to react with surprise, maybe with fear, I don't know, because what he gave me was neutral, like it's every day that some bleary-eyed frenzied motherfucker from the City walks into his Avis office at 2am. Either that or he looked at me like I was beige. Beige is the most boring color in the world. Not light, not dark, not emotional, just beige. This dude was looking at me like I was beige.

"Look man, I don't know why you're here but I got no money. My guy deposited it earlier and I got like three bucks on me. I got no credit cards because I'm poor as shit and I work at Avis. I'm here because I got no money for an apartment and I have to live at home with my mom and five kids. And I don't want to go home because it sucks. So whatever you want, you should just take your ass out that door because I got nothing and I don't give a fuck."

And in six sentences he had told me his life story. My kindred spirit. Before answering I looked around at the office. Spartan and filled with shitty paperwork or some clutter, but in one corner I saw a sleeping bag, a pillow, a water jug with a heating element and three boxes of ramen in a cup. There was also a copy of Ellison's *Invisible Man* next to the ramen.

"Hey look, I'm not here to rob you. And I'm sorry I busted in. I need a car. I'm late and my flight just got in and I gotta drive almost four hours. I saw the light…" And I trailed off after that because I could hear my own voice and it sounded ridiculously lame.

"Dude, we're closed. I do not work after 12am. I'm here because I'm here. I'll open again in a few hours but right now I'm about to go to sleep."

I plopped down into the open chair across from his desk. Every office always has an open chair. It's a confessional. You only sit in it if you've got something to say.

"Ok, let me start. I'm from New York. My mom died yesterday but I only found out from my sister today. She's in trouble and there's no one to take care of her. She's, well, she's kind of sick and my mom was the one to deal with her. I was supposed to land right before midnight, but we got delayed out of O'Hare. I'm hungry, I'm tired, I'm worried, and I'm just trying to get home. I need help. And right now, you're the only guy who can provide it."

It sounded like some goddamn speech from a movie, the turning point where people come from two different worlds to celebrate their shared humanity. I hate that shit. It's corny. Real life doesn't work that way. We're messy, remember?

But it got weirder and a little more like screen life. The guy looked at me funny, kind of turning his head to size me up. He reached down into his desk and pulled out a set of keys, throwing them in one smooth motion. I was so surprised they hit me in the chest and fell into my lap.

"Look man, you are the only dude in the last two weeks who's been honest with me. I hear all kinds of bullshit all day, from customers, from my workers, from those other folks renting cars at other companies. I provide a service and no one gives a fuck. You got a real problem and I can solve it. That's a company car." He pointed at the keys that still sat in my lap. "We all got one of those, something to get us from place to place, an emergency car, something for 'just in case'. Well, this is just in case. Take the car. I know you won't steal it." And that was it.

He stared at me. I stared back and shifted around uncomfortably. I mean, this guy was giving me a free car. He didn't know my name, he had no idea if I was fucking looney tunes, but he did it anyway.

"Don't say anything. Just take it."

"Thank you." It came out small. But it was perhaps the very first time in my life when those two words weren't perfunctory. Sure, I'd said thanks before, but it was mostly just an obligation.

You know, when someone gets the door and you say *thank you* because if you don't, you'll look like a dick, but you don't really care all that much if someone opened the door in the first place, like you could have gotten it yourself?

"Thank you." I said it again but this time louder and looking this stranger right in the eye.

"It's OK. I don't want this to be like all teary and shit, but I've asked for lots of help and I've been turned down so many times I'm kind of used to it. But it doesn't mean that I've got to turn it down. Right? Someone asks for help, I help. Pretty simple. You need this and I can provide it. So why shouldn't I?"

Even my inner cynic couldn't reject that. Maybe it was something I needed to practice myself.

Silence again for a few seconds. I kept turning the keys over and over in my fingers.

"What's your name?" I finally spat out.

"Dylan Axelrod. Mom was a Bob Dylan fan, God knows why. Motherfucker can't sing and he's a white Jewish dude. I'm black, raised Baptist, closing in on agnosticism, and like N.W.A. and Dr. Dre, old school, you know?"

"I'm Jack, Jack Francis of the Oklahoma Francis clan. Dylan does suck. I like EDM, John Coltrane, and Stevie Ray Vaughn. I'm a chef in New York City and with you on the whole agnostic thing."

"Coltrane, yeah Coltrane. That dude can play the horn. Good shit."

And it was silent again as we both played some Coltrane in our heads. "I gotta get going."

"Yeah, no problem. I gotta get to sleep. Car is in the lot for Avis, space A-1. Tank's full. To get out of the lot at this time of night just punch in 2018, like this year. We change it every year. Bring it back when you're done. I ain't going nowhere. I work six days a week, wander on the seventh, and then come back here to get ready for the next six."

With that, I got up. We shook hands, I mumbled thanks again, and turned to leave, our quiet moment of humanity crumbling away.

I was on the road ten minutes later. The car was a late model Lexus. Not bad for an emergency car. Not bad at all. Once on the highway I put the cruise on eighty and just pointed it in the right direction. I plugged in my phone and of course had to listen to Lady Bird. My man Dylan. Not Bob. Axelrod.

Exactly three hours and fifty minutes later I had arrived at the farm. Even though cruise control had helped, I still had to stop and slow down in those God-awful small towns with their blinking red lights as two-lane highways become Main Street and then highway again as you depart the sparkling metropolis. The turnoff south of Kiowa, Kansas and across the state line in Oklahoma is like every other turnoff for miles, indistinguishable and non-descript. There's a house and a barn and a dirt road that goes nowhere. But somehow the old instincts kicked in where I needed to turn, exactly six miles south of Kiowa, seven miles from the border. It had been years since I'd been back but it didn't matter. It's a DNA thing, somehow imprinted on our genes.

On the corner were the Millers. I never really knew them except for seeing them at church now and then growing up. They were about twenty years older than my mom and seemed fucking ancient. I wondered if they were still kicking. The car in the drive looked the same, a mid-80's Dodge sedan, not one of those sleek little things, but one that was literally twice the size of most cars now. Man, those farmers can live forever, Oklahoma fountain of youth and all that shit.

Another mile down from that was the Obramawicz family. Now they were cool. Daddy Obramawicz farmed–yeah, surprise there–but he also grew a little weed out back and would share now and then with the middle-aged crowd. He had some hippie in him I'm told, Berkeley in the late 60's. He claimed to have been at Haight-Ashbury.

Maybe so, because that guy had some sweet weed and totally loved Jimi Hendrix. His off-the-side business never made waves. I think it's 'cause the county sheriff was his buddy and rumor was he toked it up a bit as well.

Mom Obramawicz ran a Montessori preschool in Kiowa. How the hell that worked I'll never know. That bunch of small-town hicks couldn't spell Montessori let alone knew what it was. But the only other preschool in town was run by an old lady who could barely hear and bitched about being with kids. Go figure, a preschool teacher who hated children. So the choice was between an angry hag or some nice woman doing some weird shit in preschool. They chose weird. And people started to like it. They even liked the vegan diet she prepped for the kids' meals. Mom and Dad Obramawicz only had one kid of their own – maybe a preschool was enough – and she was smokin' hot. Jennifer Elizabeth Obramawicz, four years older than me, and gave me my first legitimate hard-on. I was twelve, maybe thirteen, bored as shit one day and trying to figure out what to do. When that happened, we would usually wander over to the train tracks or down to the creek that divided our land from the Obramawicz place. So there I am twiddling my thumbs and along comes Jenny. She doesn't see me, so I hide under a bush, maybe twenty feet away. She's down by the creek and starts to take off her clothes. Not all quick, but very delicate, like a high-class striptease. She gets down to the bra and panties and I am blown away. Look, at this point in my life all I've ever seen are the white granny panties and huge nylon brown bras my mom wears. A) my mom is not attractive and B) my mom's lingerie is really not fucking attractive. I had an ex-girlfriend once who wore those panties at select times. She called them her "go furthers", as in, "when I wear these panties you need to go further away because you are not getting any bedroom exercise tonight."

So Jenny O is in these beautiful tight panties, black with pink trim, high cut so you can see the inner thigh, with just a little bit of her tight ass sticking out. Her bra was nothing but a little lace, and at sixteen or seventeen, she had an unbelievable rack. Yep, rock hard, I was. But then came the *coup de grace*. Bra and panties came off and then she went to skinny dip in the creek, sun streaming behind her, hair all wet, shaking it out, dribbling water over her skin, a real *Fast Times at Ridgemont High* moment where the hot chick gets out of the pool naked for Judge Reinhold.

At this point I completely fell over the bush I was hiding behind. But Jenny, cool as they come, only glanced my way, caught my eye, and just kept doing what she was doing. Damn, that girl had it going on. So of course I did what any red-blooded male would do. I ran like hell. I'd been caught and when that happens you get the hell out. Or so we think in adolescence. I saw Jenny a lot after that, school and in town, and she never said a thing. After we'd both grown up, I saw her at the Wal- Mart in Alva. I was in my late twenties at this point, just passing through on my way to NYC, a real man of the world. We hadn't seen each other for a few years but I was rushing to get something or other, I went past the lingerie aisle and there she was looking at panties and bras. She glanced up, smiled and said, "Remember?" Instantly the same reaction in my nether regions. And I ran like hell again.

Once you get past the Obramawicz place it's only a few paces down the road where you go over a steep rise to the train tracks. Once you cross those, you're on our land. Down from the train tracks, across the creek bridge, and twenty feet beyond, just past the copse of oak trees, is the turn into our house.

The house is plain, but I know every inch of it. As you come up the dirt drive it sits on another rise, maybe fifty feet back from the road. The first thing you see is a wide front porch, tucked away and protected by the low roof. I spent a lot of hours there, just sitting, listening to my mom talk to folks, mostly Uncle Ray from down the road. I would go out there by myself to whittle sometimes. I know, Andy Griffith and Mayberry shit, but it's like a rite of passage in the country. Some old fart has to sit on the front porch with his dog at his feet as he shows you how to use knife and stick. "When I was young" or "Back in my day" - it seems to start the same every time, but you know we have stereotypes for a reason.

As you get closer to the house the drive takes you past the west side of the structure; if you kept following that drive it would loop around a line of trees and take you back to the road. But at the tip of the loop, past those trees where we usually park, you see the whole expanse of our farm. The barn is fifty paces to the north, cow pasture just to the right of that, musty garage and storage area for the tractors and other farm implements, and then the chicken coop just to the right of that, maybe twenty feet away.

Attached to the chicken coop-barely-is my basketball hoop. Uncle Ray thought the hoop might distract me after my dad died, but he also understood the coop was the only place possible to receive the glow of the house lights late at night. Boys with a lot of pent-up sadness might need to shoot hoops in the early hours just to work out the hardness of life. And I did, for years on end, really. I got pretty decent at basketball. I was a starting guard on a team that finished second at state; it was the smallest classification of schools in Oklahoma, but I still averaged close to twenty points a game and got some scholarship offers from small schools in the area.

I parked near the chicken coop just to look at the hoop. That rusty thing was still there, warped and literally hanging by one screw. No one had bothered to put it back right. On the other hand, who would use it? I wandered over to the side door, the real "entrance" to our house. See, most people would park over this direction and not in front by the porch. They would go through the screen door, past the cistern, and right into the kitchen. Maybe that's where I got my sensibilities. The kitchen was always the heart of our home. Not the living room and not the porch. Always the kitchen.

When I walked in it was like stepping back in time. I hadn't been here for years, but nothing had changed. Didn't surprise me. The same solid oak table, red vinyl-covered chairs around it, table chipped in the corner, a scar running down the middle from when I had decided to carve a long filet of beef without protection. To the left was the stove, your basic white four burner electric with a cast iron pan on top. Beyond that the lime green counter with the sink in the middle, same dishes stretched down the side, cupboards neatly aligned along the wall, pointing to the pantry where my sister stored all her crazy shit. Same old, same old.

I wandered past the table and into the living room, illuminated by the soft light of a lamp in the corner. For as long as I could remember, Mom had always left a lamp on. She said she wanted to make sure people found their way in the dark if they had to get up, but I think maybe she didn't like the dark much at all after Dad died. One couch and two easy chairs, recliners of course, surrounded the couch and pointed to the console TV. A veritable "Father Knows Best" living room, all 1950's and shit.

But there was one thing different. A woman was tucked, literally, into the couch, as if she were trying to curl into a ball and protect herself from the pains of waking life. Her face was pushed into the cushions so I couldn't see who it was, but her hair was shoulder length, a pretty, dirty blonde in the dim light coming through the window, and from my view the ass and body were superb. Hey, I'm still a guy. It's what we examine from the back every time. I stood there contemplating her but also trying to figure out who this might be and why she was here in this house. I had thought Ray was going to be around.

But I think we all have an intuition when someone is examining us, even in our deepest sleep, and this woman began to stir and uncoil from her protective fetal position. She turned her head to face me. Somehow she recognized me, maybe it was because she was expecting me, but the face was still a mystery. Soft features, maybe early to mid-30's, pretty eyes, small mouth, but a face that could express real well. I know because even in the moment of waking she had gone from sleep-eyed zombie to surprised to apprehensive joy at seeing me. She smiled, but it was hesitant, which said *I'm glad to see you but this is kind of weird and is it OK for me to be here?*

"Hey Jack, how are you? And what time is it?"

Soft voice to match the soft face. And none of this gravelly, I-just-woke-up-after-three-shots-and-two-beers-last-night voice. A soothing, inviting voice.

"I'm OK, tired. Who are you?" It seemed like the right question to ask, but it came out angrily. I could see her face change from soft to guarded.

"Beth Schwartzer. Ray's daughter?"

It was the perfect intonation, the one that said, "I'm Beth, Ray's daughter, you fucking dense asshole." But I was in no mood to be peaceful. Too tired, too tense about this whole mess. I let the silence sit while I thought about the next step in my interrogation.

"And why are you here?" But what I really wanted to say was, *Oh my God, I haven't seen you in forever and you look great and I really appreciate you being here for my wack-job sister.* Again, too tired and too tense.

She let the silence sit between us. I think she was pondering how to deal with me. Two can play at this game.

"Your sister was struggling. She asked me to stay until you got back. I think she feels really lost but doesn't know how to say it. I..." She hesitated because she was starting to change from tough-ass bitch to something softer. "I'm sorry about your mom. I know this is tough and it's early. But I'm sorry and I hope I can help somehow."

I ignored her calming voice.

"No, why are you HERE, like in Oklahoma? Don't you live in Maryland or Delaware or somewhere?"

What an ass. It's six in the morning, Mom's dead, sister's asleep in the other room and I'm asking why this woman who clearly is as kind as she is beautiful is in Oklahoma. I haven't seen her in forever, but I have a fleeting image of her rejecting me when we were kids, something about another boyfriend. I'm too pissed for Proustian clarity and remembrance.

The dark cloud covered her face again and disappeared just as quickly. An intake of breath and she was back to being calm and almost apologetic.

"Look, I really am sorry and this is hard. I'm here because I was visiting Ray, just hanging out for a while and trying to gather myself. When your mom died, I came over with him and then stayed to talk with your sister while he made arrangements. I'm here to help so if you're back now I'll take off. I'll be around if you need anything later. And I live in Ohio now."

She made to get up and go, grabbing her bag from the side of the couch, trying to get around me towards the kitchen and an exit. As she moved that way I followed her.

In that moment, the memory returned. It was when we were teenagers, maybe fourteen or fifteen, and my hormones were just kicking in. I noticed her, like really noticed her, for the first time in all her girliness. She was back for a short visit to Ray's and I hadn't seen her in a couple of years. I remembered sharing a Coke on the front porch and my hand creeping over to touch hers. It was a fucking Rockwell painting except that as soon as I touched flesh she recoiled. She immediately said she couldn't be my girlfriend because she already had a boyfriend at home. She ran inside. That was it, the last time I saw her. Until now.

"Hey, Beth!" She stopped at the door. "I'm sorry. No excuses, just apologizing. I really appreciate you being here for my sister. It was just a surprise, you, here, and it's been forever. And I think I've had enough surprises in the last few hours that maybe this one put me over the top."

It was an apologetic ramble, but it must have sounded authentic because her shoulders relaxed and she turned around to face me.

"I get it. So, surprise! It's me!" We both chuckled. "I really meant it. If you need help with anything, please let me know. I'm at Ray's for a while more and you know how to get a hold of me. Ray's kind of shook but wants to be the man of the household." She paused. She reached out her hands to take mine and gave them a friendly squeeze.

"Beth, that is the very best thing someone has said to me today. Let's try this again later. I'd like to hear about you and life and Maryland."

"Ohio!" she laughed.

"Yeah, Ohio. So, thanks and have a good night or morning or whatever it is."

"See you later."

And with that, our hands released and she stepped out. No car, just walking home. I could have been chivalrous and offered to walk her home, but you really don't need protecting on a dirt road in the middle of Oklahoma at 6am. She was going to be just fine.

And maybe I was going to be OK too, now.

7

JILL

I woke up at my normal time, hungry like always, but ready to "attack the day!" I like that, attack the day, because it somehow makes every day a battle, but like a fun battle to see what you can get out of it. And if you win, you get to be happy and your dreams are sweet! Except my dreams were kind of strange last night. After talking to Beth, I tried to sleep but was real restless. I could hear her out in the living room watching some old Western movie. It sounded like High Noon with Gary Cooper but I wasn't sure. Anyways, I didn't need to go check on her because I could hear it.

Somewhere around a gunfight scene I must have drifted off because suddenly I was in the gunfight myself, trapped in this alleyway in a big city, wanting to get out but not having to shoot the guy at the other end of the street. Actually it wasn't two guys but it was my brother and my mom. Both of them had guns and were smiling at me like wild dogs I had seen once on the Discovery Channel. So I had to, like, shoot them to get out. I shot my mom and she just looked up at me and said "Good, finally some peace!" I tried to shoot my brother too, but he just kept dodging the bullets, this way and that way, up and down, he could even move his body like a superhero, just barely missing the bullet. One time everything slowed down to slow-motion. So cool. There he was almost about to be hit but he moved his upper body out of the way with this cool spinning move, kind of like in The Matrix. I totally love that movie, it's like a dream within a dream. Are you awake or sleeping? Alive or dead? So in my dream Jack is avoiding all my bullets but he's not shooting back. Suddenly the sun comes out over our alleyway and he looks at me and says, "All you need to do is turn around and walk out of here." And that's when I woke up. Weird.

I dragged myself into the kitchen and what to my wandering eyes should appear (a miniature sleigh? NO! but Jack! He was sitting at the table drinking coffee, crappy coffee, by the smell of it, and just staring out the back window that looks down on the creek.

"Hi Jack!" I said it all bubbly because I knew it was going to be a great day! Jack was back and now I wasn't going to be alone anymore! Furthermore, he could get to the store and stock our pantry. We were out of everything of course.

He got up kind of slowly and moved towards me. He opened up his arms and took me in a real slow hug. It felt weird cause Jack hadn't really ever hugged me. So it was a hug but kind of not a hug, like it was foreign to both of us, real hesitant and such.

He released me and stepped back. "You doing Ok?"

"Sure, a little hungry but OK. Is Beth still here?"

"No, she left when I got here. She said she'd be back later to check on you, maybe bring some things over."

"Good, cause we need food in this place. Can we get breakfast now?"

He looked a little stunned like he was amazed that I wanted

the first meal of the day. I know, I know, Mom had just died and maybe we needed to chat, but we've all got to eat.

"I tell you what. Why don't you let me make some breakfast for us. It'll help clear my mind from the trip and maybe we can talk while I cook. You can tell me what happened to Mom, where things are, all of it. Sound good?"

"Yes." I know I was grinning because here in my own house was a real live chef who was about to make us breakfast. Super awesome!

But what followed meal-wise was a major disappointment. I wanted hollandaise and Canadian bacon or maybe a frittata with wild greens or even your basic baguette sandwich. But did I get this? No, I got pancakes. Measly pancakes. But in his defense, all he could find in the kitchen was one egg and some flour, although there were some nice strawberry preserves to put on top. While he ladled the batter onto the sizzling griddle, he asked again how I was doing.

"Good, just like the last time you asked five minutes ago."

"No, I mean how are you with all of this? What happened to Mom? Ray only said she was gone and it was natural, whatever that means."

"Well," I hesitated cause I was thinking about how to present this. "I woke up late and Mom wasn't up already. I checked on her, but she kept sleeping. And it stunk because I had to get breakfast but as you can see there wasn't much. I kept checking but she kept sleeping. Until finally I checked on her and she was dead as a doornail. And then I called you."

"So that's it? Like was she feeling badly the day before she died? Was she upset? Was anything wrong?"

What was this, the third degree? Sheesh. I didn't know much. Mom really never said much to me other than to ask what I needed at the store. One time I had tried to tell her about Dr. Phil's show but she told me she really wasn't interested and that she would just read her book. So we didn't talk much.

"Nope, nothing wrong. Well, she said she was tired and didn't really want to go to the store, but otherwise she seemed fine. Running errands, going to the doctor, the usual stuff."

"Doctor? Why?"

"I don't know why. She just went to the doctor every couple weeks. Didn't you talk to her?"

"Jill, I have no idea what she told you but we hadn't really talked in ten years. The last time was when I came through here when I was moving from Portland to New York. And you remember how that turned out, right?"

Boy, did I remember. Not the particulars of course, but I remembered. Lots of yelling and screaming and I even heard my name loads of times but I retreated to my room. I remembered the door slamming and then Mom coming to my room to say Jack was gone and wouldn't be back. Jack wrote me after that saying he was sorry he hadn't said goodbye and that he would write often. He was good about it for a while but then it kind of dwindled to just Christmas and birthday cards. But it was cool cause he would usually send me something awesome like an autographed cookbook or maybe a cool kitchen tool that Mom couldn't find on her shopping trips.

There was silence as he kept working on the pancakes. "So why'd you come back then?"

More silence. I was starting to get uncomfortable. I mean, Mom didn't talk to me much but then we were simpatico, you know? She had her books, I had my TV and my cooking. But here Jack and me were in the same space and he wasn't saying much.

"I came back because I'm obligated." He said it softly like

there was some angry in it, maybe a little hissing through the teeth. I knew that one. Our daddy before he died did the same thing with me whenever I got into something I shouldn't have. I learned real quick to avoid it.

"Why obligated? Ray could help me out. I mean, I know I called you all scared and stuff but when I thought about it I knew I would be fine."

"No, you are not!" This time the hissing was gone and Jack was right in front of me. The pancakes were burning. I smelled them.

"Jill, I may not care much if Mom died or not, but I do worry about you a lot. Remember when Dad died? You took care of me. I was a scared little eight-year-old who didn't know what to do. Mom had checked out and you were the only one who got me through it. You did it for me, now I gotta do it for you."

I was ready to get out of this conversation quick. Dad's death was really hard and dredged up some bad memories. I just kept quiet. Sometimes that's the best way to escape.

"Look!" Jack was almost yelling now. "Mom was gone a lot and you took care of me. But then Mom checked back in and she was a fucking bitch. Nothing worked. And so with two moms, you and her both, I had to leave. I knew it at fourteen but I had to wait four more years to take off. Those were the worst four years of my life. And at thirty-eight, I still can't let it go. But I also want to help you."

That was kind of cool. I think maybe Jack was saying he loved me. So I asked.

"You love me, don't you?" It came out kind of giddy. It was a total Love Boat scene.

"Yeah Jill. I love every bit of your forty-two-year-old ass."

But there was this really big smile on his face.

There was more silence now but I didn't need to escape. Jack got the pancakes and brought them over to me. He sat down across from me and asked the BIG question. You know, there's always a question that has to be asked in those dramas on TV. Like, "Should we get married?" or "Who were you with last night?" Yep, it was BIG question time.

"So what do we do now, Jill? I live and work in New York and don't want to leave. You could…come with me…" His voice trailed off like he was asking a question, the up- turn in his voice right at the end. I bet he was thinking about going back to New York City, maybe, hopefully wishing it might happen. But I cut him off.

"You know I can't do that, silly." I was trying to lighten what had become a really tense situation again. "I live here and can't think about going out."

But my ploy didn't work because he kept on.

"Sure, we can make it work. Like, maybe we could drug you and then when you woke up you'd be in New York City. I've got a great place, you already know Derek, or maybe we could get something a little bigger for all three of us. And I could get you all the ingredients you needed. I could go to Little Italy or Chinatown or wherever. It's all there Jill. You could do it."

But that's when I started to get testy, no more quiet escape. Ok, I was getting freaked out. My voice came out all angry and creaky at the same time.

"You know I can't go. Just thinking about it makes me all scared inside. New York is cool and all and the food would be great but I cannot - CANNOT! - go out. Drugs or no drugs, I know what moving means. So I'm here to stay, like it or not. This is my home."

I guess at that point I could have been all drama queen and got up and slammed the door to my room. But I didn't. I stayed right there and ate my pancakes. And they were real good.

Jack tried one more time. "Then what are we going to do Jill? You have to stay here and I have to go home. So where do we go?"

And that was that. I didn't have an answer. I finished my food, set the dishes on the counter, and went back to my room. I sat up on my bed and thought a little about moving. I know, it seems crazy but there are those times when we dream about doing something or being somebody else but we can't. Like flying. Or being a billionaire and having whatever you wanted for every single meal of the day. I told my mom about one of my ideas one day and she said, "Honey, you may think you want to run off with the circus, but in the end reality hits and you're left standing where you are." I didn't get it then because I hadn't said I wanted to join the circus. I mean, really, who would want to join a smelly circus. The food is all hot dogs and popcorn and it really stinks when you walk around the animals. I had told my mom that I wanted to go to Paris and visit Julia Child's home and then get an apartment and learn to cook like she did. No three-ring circus there. But when I asked my mom again she was a little madder at me. "Honey, you are dreaming. You can't go anywhere." And then under her breath I heard a small hiss that sounded like "And neither can I."

But irregardless (I love that word … I picked it up on Will and Grace) I still sat dreaming about New York City. Ok, it wasn't Paris but wow it would be so cool. Food and people and culture. So different from dry and dusty Oklahoma. What would it be like to go down Broadway or maybe go to a new Daniel Boulud restaurant on 69th Street?

Oh my God, I was wiggly with excitement.

But then I heard Jack's car pull out of the drive and reality set back in. Jack was leaving. I was not. I couldn't. My circus would never appear.

8

JACK

I had to get out of there. No, actually I needed some fucking sleep. Two hours wasn't cutting it, and it was the same Jill, the same response, the same shit that had pushed me out when I was eighteen. It was Jill's limitations, her inability to go anywhere at all when all I wanted to do was go *everywhere*.

Once Mom checked out - not like her recent death but more like when Dad died and her "event" happened - Jill tried to be the *de facto* mother. I mean I was eight when Dad died and then Mom's depression went into overdrive for the next four years. Jill was my caretaker at that point, but Christ it got tougher. Maybe it was me just growing up and adding a little more testosterone in my bloodstream. I am a bit of a hellion at heart and that certainly didn't help in my dealings with Jill. Jesus, by the time I was eighteen I could barely stand to be around her. I only talked to Mom for the bare essentials like when I needed money or asking what time we were having dinner. It was pretty lonely.

Mix that with my anger and my hell boy and I was pretty much fucking gone the day after I graduated from high school.

So here I was twenty years later, 2018, with the same shitty feelings bubbling up and I had to get out. But on a Monday in rural Oklahoma where would I go? I didn't feel like checking in with Ray yet, and maybe I just wasn't ready to see Beth again so that was out. The back roads around our farm went on for miles, each quarter section more dusty than the next, but they were hard and straight lines cut into the Earth to get from one wheat field to the next. Houses dotted the landscape. The Burns family lived two miles to the north, the Cosgroves just a mile east of them. Good families both, each helping us when Dad died, even checking in through the years. We returned the favor when tragedy struck and took Mr. Burns and Mrs. Cosgrove in farm accidents. Man, that was a dark-ass time around here. I didn't know whether to be envious or disgusted that they had stayed locked to the land and never moved on. I kept drifting north and east.

There was the Sutter place, the Dowds, the Carlsons, June Smith and Esther Lingerfeldt, maybe gay and maybe not, but after the rumors stood down and they kept on being upstanding members of the church, no one seemed to give a shit.

Just past their place found me on the outskirts of Kiowa. Kiowa is like every other small farm town in Kansas and Oklahoma. Towns like this are plopped down, just kind of there. I always wondered why, but the best answer I ever got was from some old fart who seemed to have lived in one small town or another forever. He told me it was about distance and only distance. Towns like this were created by the owners of farm stores, the ones that supplied seed and fertilizer and the tools for all the farmers trying to suck a life from the land. These shopkeepers basically set up at a place that seemed to be the right distance from their clients. Get too far away from the bulk of them and you didn't have enough business. Get too close to any one of them and the farmers got pissed because you were encroaching on their space. These shopkeepers had to find the soft spot, not too far, not too close, and when they hit it just right other business followed. The bank, the school, obviously the damn church, all of it, until you had a town and had to name it something other than "Place of the Feed and Supply Store".

There was no trace of a central supply store in Kiowa anymore…or at least one that was the hub of Main Street. Actually there were now two stores of that nature, one on either side of town. Ironically, they were run by the same guy but kept different store names, "Kiowa Feed and Supply" on the north end of town and "Kiowa Farm Store" to the south. The layout was the same in both, the products were identical, but there was always a fierce loyalty to one or the other depending on where you lived.

Separating the two was a broad Main Street, crowned in the middle and curving to the sidewalks so that when the torrential summer rains came water would run down to the gutters. Parking spaces lined either side, big enough for those enormous farm trucks everyone seemed to own. Those things get like eight miles to the gallon but are somehow necessary. Necessary my ass. It's about ego and dick size. I always thought that it was an inverse relationship. The bigger the truck, the smaller the dick and the more insecure the man. The smaller the truck…well, you get it.

Main Street even now was lined with trucks as the farmers got a start to the day and the week. As you moved from one end of town to the other, it really was like stepping back in time. Storefronts with large windows, big stenciled letters scrambled across window panes announcing the wares for sale inside. The clothing store, the diner, the bank, the toy store, the sewing and knitting emporium, another coffee shop, groceries...but fuck, no liquor store. That's what sounded good right now. I'm no alkie, but I'd just flown halfway across the god-damned country, met some stranger from a half-life ago, and had to deal with my closed-in and frustrating sister. A little bourbon, even at 10am, might have taken the edge off.

Down the side streets from all those storefronts were the churches and, God! - no pun intended - were there a lot of them. Methodist, Baptist, Presbyterians, Second Baptists, Anabaptists, Regular Baptists, Normal Baptists, and the Ecumenical Church of Christ America on a stick. Ok, that last one doesn't exist, but maybe it could here in the Heartland. I mean, I know my mom and sister were the catalyst for driving me away at eighteen, but this awful, stifling town with its faux community faith-and-family bullshit just pushed me over the edge. See everyone, I mean everyone, goes to church in this town. Well, except the atheists and the Catholics. The one group are heathens, the other is a bunch of freaky cult motherfuckers–well, not to me–but in this town you are ostracized if you publicly fall into one of those camps. I made the mistake of asking our pastor at the Methodist church whether there was a God when I was eight and my dad died.

Instead of comfort I got yelled at like I was the root of all evil. He wondered how I could question God's existence. "There is always a God," he said, "and He has taken your father to a better place."

"Yeah, but why would God do that?" I asked.

"Because he can" is the answer I got back.

And that was it. Finito, end game. At eight maybe I should have been scared and hunkered down to learn more. But instead I got pissed. At twelve, during a Sunday school lesson I told my teacher this was all bullshit. I even said that word. Mom punished me to holy hell but I could give a fuck. At fourteen, I just refused to go. Mom tried. but I said I didn't want to and didn't believe. I found out later she was in tears that day and the same fucked-up pastor, trying to comfort her found out my dirty secret of unbelief. Rather than give my mom a hug and say it was OK, he turned that same bullshit on her. "Better get him right with The Lord," he said, "or you're going to hell with him." From that day forward we never went back to that church or any church. Mom even threw out the Bibles and the nifty little needlepoint New Testament quotes that had dotted the wall of our house. Yeah, no longer having Mark 4:20 on my walls was a big hit to my ego but I survived. I think I put a Jimi Hendrix poster or some shit up to cover the shadowed wood where the Jesus quote had been.

9

BETH

Ray said he needed a few things at the store and I happily volunteered to go. I needed the drive. No, that wasn't it. I needed a release. Maybe it was a release from Ray's sadness. That's my habit, always attempting to flee from emotion. At least, that was the narrative a therapist in my 20's had put in my head. Without a father to anchor to in my life, she pontificated, you are adrift. And when emotion arises without an anchor, the attempt is to flee emotionally and physically. I fled her Freudian crap shortly thereafter. But maybe she was onto something. I had fled relationships for most of my adult life. I had fled my mother and her disastrous life of excess and failed romance, first to college and then to graduate school where I immersed myself in the most sanitized, logical, and emotionless discipline I could find: Sweet, abiding philosophy.

Maybe this trip to Oklahoma was a fleeing as well, a removal from my sanitized life as a scholar and researcher. Research in philosophy is different from chemistry or history. We read the old texts of wise sages and attempt to put a new spin on things, writing painfully dry articles that only a few will ever read. Even that, the very independence of scholarship and research, was emotionally removed. I didn't need to talk to anyone in that context. In that mode, I could keep my shields up and another's emotions at bay. But that life is too clean, too sanitized, too inauthentic. On the exterior, I am polished but inside I am clamoring for connection. Somehow, always needing more.

Even with that recognition, I needed to get out and away from Ray. I needed to find release. It was all too much.

God, it's pretty here. Just pretty. I don't know how to say it more simply than that. At the end of spring the wheat fields are an endless stretch of green just beginning to take on a tint of gold that will turn into harvest. Up close, the fields have a life of their own, swaying and moving in undulating waves, each drying stalk dances with its mates. I know because I walked those fields over and over when I needed to flee and wasn't yet old enough to drive away. Rain is fleeting here except for the thunderstorms that will fight the very existence of those wheat fields. There is no gentleness in these storms, only this voracious hunger to destroy. Farmers know it. Ray investigates the sky each day, peering at the clouds as if they were a crystal ball that could tell the future.

From above, those same fields seem like a checkerboard, each quarter of land made distinct from the next by bisecting roads. Isn't there a song about that, Jason Aldean maybe? It's both embarrassing and beautiful that I know this but sometimes even philosophy professors need a country bar at times. My colleagues don't hang at country bars and no one is emotionally sanitized there. Maybe it's the only place I can wear my boots.

That checkerboard often has a creek or a shelter belt of trees slashing across that tiny perfect square, but it's a simple scratch along the playing board. It's like the Almighty slipped up and scraped the land like a nick on a damaged coffee table. But humanity intrudes on the landscape also when the perfect circles of pivot irrigation fill the squares,, an outline in the summer followed by a lush green circle in winter and spring. The geometry of it all is sublime.

I couldn't help but notice how different this was. My Ohio is not necessarily an urban jungle, but it's still noisy, both visually and auditorially. Cars, buildings, cement, the din of people living. More often than not, I keep my head down and my interior shut off from others. Shut it all out. Live a life away from it all. But I don't do that here. I have to notice. And open up. And become something new. Really, why was I here in Oklahoma? For a job? For healing?

I noticed only the silence and vastness and rolled my windows down, no NPR to drown out life. Better to inhale these surroundings in silence. City life can be claustrophobic, a patina of shadows from overgrown buildings pressing down on the worn pavement. But here on the Plains, vistas open up and I can see. I see out there ten and twenty miles beyond but I can also see what's right in front of me. It also demands acknowledgement. The pebbles on the road, the dust leaking out behind, the sway of row after row of wheat. The air is different, sweet with the scents of spring, no taint of human pollution. I see telephone poles, fixed totems of a rural lifeline to power and communication set exactly one hundred feet apart. No cell towers here, at least not yet.

As I approached Kiowa, the dirt turned to pavement, the road gently sweeping over a short hill, Bonderman's Hill–named after some famous citizen who did some famous thing at some famous time–and I spied the structures of middling civilization. There was the water tower, like a beacon announcing "You have arrived Somewhere." But where was I? Physically, I knew, but it was a bigger question, really. Isn't it funny the way the Plains have a way of stretching us out, making us more aware because of the silences and the vastness of it all?

I turned my attention to Jack at that moment. It's not clear why he entered my mind as I was pondering these big questions.

Jack.

I remembered Jack as a friend. As a kid. We were equals and it made no difference if he was a boy and I was a girl. We were just the same age and you found friends wherever you could. Mostly we played at Ray's house. I would ask him sometimes if we could go over to his house or maybe play in the barn there, but he would say his mom was tired or his sister was weird. Maybe I knew even then he was trying to keep me away from something. I just didn't know what. Ray finally told me the full story after I graduated from college.

It all changed with Jack when we were teenagers. I was back for a few weeks in the "summer of my becoming", which was what Mom called puberty. Becoming a woman with my first period, becoming more independent from my mother, becoming angry at the world. It's that time of life–really, any young girl's life–where it all makes no sense. Hormones, reality, people–none of it.

Remember the movie Lady Bird with Saorsie Ronan? I saw it a few times in the theater because that character of Lady Bird was me. Angry at my mother but wanting connection from her. Angry at my father for not being there. Wanting to fit in anywhere because in New York I was that awkward hick from Oklahoma and in Oklahoma I was some nouvelle city slicker. That summer, I just wanted to be Jack's friend again, that equal, like when we were younger kids. But he reached out to hold my hand when we were on the front porch and I panicked. I ran away. I never spoke to him again. Maybe I wanted that friend again. It wasn't that I didn't have a friend in New York but I wanted the friend that knew me best, all of me. That was on my mind.

There was some romance in my life. The departed chef I had mentioned to Jill. A long-term relationship with another PhD student in history. But when it came time to commit to something more than just the convenience of being in the same place for school, I realized he was just there, kind of a dandy and always smug, an East Coast elitist who made fun of my Oklahoma background. He hated my boots. I realized that he had brought his prep school and Ivy League education to his doctoral studies in the Midwest and it was all just bullshit. He framed his snobby attitudes and resentments as a liberal fight against the oppressive corporatism of a dominant white culture. It played well with his academic friends and his doctoral mentors but it clashed with the Midwest ethos of the town. I attended a rally with him about some restrictive town ordinance–bathrooms or pesticides or wages, really they're all the same to people who thrive on their own righteousness–and he got into a physical fight with a townie and got arrested. He wore it as a badge of honor and announced it in his classes. He loved the adulation. I thought he was an ass. It wasn't authentic. Instead it was a game, a charade, a disguise. He was playing the part of an aggrieved elitist academic who needed to take a position against "the man" even though he was the man himself.

So, I fled.

But Jack. Jack seems what, real? I haven't seen him for more than five minutes and already I appreciate his anger, his smile, his chuckle. There is no game there. And I'm lonely. Perhaps for a friend, perhaps for something more. Definitely for something different than I currently have. It's even more complicated because it's not just the release and not just Ray that brings me here. I'm here to interview for a job at the local regional state college. They want someone to take on an immense teaching load of general education courses, maybe a philosophy course or two, but also something in literature and history, maybe in religion. It is the absolute dregs of academia. The pay is horrible. The load is horrible. It's career suicide. But I think I want it. It's more authentic than what I'm doing now. I would be with students. That scares me but it feels right.

In all this reverie, I find myself in the parking lot of the IGA in Kiowa. Basic storefront with a few handcrafted signs in the windows advertising bananas and canned pintos on sale. Same with the chuck roast for the amazingly low price of $2.59 per pound. Is that good? I shop at Kroeger's and I get what I need which is usually meagre and always basic. Chicken breasts, rice, vegetables. I'm in, I'm out, that's all.

We need dinner tonight, so I thought pasta. Ray likes pasta. I found the right aisle, grabbed the spaghetti noodles closest to me and then wandered over to the jarred sauce. Ragu? Sure, I've heard of that. I turn around and almost run into him.

"I'm sorry!" I sputtered out.

"It's ... Beth?"

Sometimes the universe answers our questions.

10

JACK

Goddammit I needed to get out. Jill, fuckin' Jill. Her and this damn place. Too many memories conjured up, old habits submerged for so long and brought to the top. What was I doing here? I know it's unkind with Mom's death and Jill's condition, but fuck them both. What do I need to deal with them and their shit?

So I ran. Somewhere. Anywhere but here. But here is always present. And in Oklahoma and the borderlands of Kansas, here just keeps going and going. Wheat fields, dirt roads, narrow paved byways with only silence and vistas for friends. But maybe it's not so terrible. I mean, I've been thinking about getting out of NYC for a while now. The job sucks and I don't see myself moving over to fine dining anytime soon even if that's where the money is. My cooking is just rote memory now, never art. I want it to be creative, not some life-sucking paint-by-numbers bullshit. I'd miss Derek if I left. That's it. Living in the City is a grind. It's hard, way too fuckin' hard. I want some softness in my life. A woman. I don't know. Maybe. But they're hard too. Relationships are hard. The starting, the ending, the boredom in between.

I need a new "here". But not here in Oklahoma. Never here, right? How could it ever be here, with the nothingness of it all? What fills this place?

Kiowa, Kansas fills this place. I drove by instinct, again, and ended up in Kiowa, population 1016, a grid of streets in perfect calculus. I got on 7th Street by habit. It would take me to the town square, of course. Everything south and north of me was numbers, 1st Street all the way to 16th and then a wheat field. But everything I passed going to the square was named. Revolutionary row – Washington Street, Adams Street, Franklin Avenue. Then the garden – Rose, Peony, Daisy, Sunflower – followed by the Ivies – Yale, Harvard, Brown, Princeton, and Cornell. Colors and birds took you right out of town, 7th Street turning into a state highway to the nether regions of southwestern Kansas. I asked Mom once why all the street names were like this. It was only the second time I ever heard her swear. "Because those hoity-toity shits who founded the place weren't very smart and thought everything back East was better." It must have been one of her fouler days with Jill.

I kept going on 7th until I hit Main Street - every small town has a Main Street - and came upon the town square. The county courthouse anchors the square and sits right inside it bordered by all four streets. It's still majestic in its own small- town-county-courthouse way. Maybe because it is the only building in the whole square bigger than two stories. I can't imagine it in NYC because it would be dwarfed, lost in a sea of skyscrapers. Here it stands out. Sidewalks crisscross the north and south lawns and park benches caress the other two sides. It hasn't changed a bit in my lifetime.

I parked the car near one of the benches and moved to sit

down, needing a pause to replenish my emotional tank. There was a mom and her two kids on a bench near mine. Mom looked pissed because Junior had dropped his ice cream and his sister, maybe a year or two older, was laughing her ass off at her brother while she polished off her rocky road, chocolate smile all aglow.

"That's fucking hilarious!"

I thought I said it to myself but like any dumbass New Yorker without a filter it popped out. New Yorkers are outwardly judgmental.

Mom looked up and glared.

"Please don't swear around my children. It's rude."

"Look lady." And I stopped. For the second time in less than twenty-four hours I checked myself. New Yorkers rarely check themselves. What was I becoming? Did I actually give a shit how I came off to this stranger or her children?

"I'm sorry. Really so very sorry. That was incredibly rude of me and I was wrong. Here, can I help you?" I scrambled to find a napkin, anything, really, to assist with this mess.

"No, thank you. We're fine. Just a day in my life." She didn't smile. She picked up her things and turned her attentions to the kiddos gawking at me.

Instead of lingering, I began to walk around the square. An antique shop, then a law office. I remembered from twenty years ago. I peered in and it looked like he hadn't updated a thing. Past that, an empty storefront and a woman's clothing store. One of the others used to be a full-service clothing store and it was where Mom had bought me school clothes, usually just t-shirts from the 80's and jeans in husky size. I was a fat kid then.

But the store at the corner of the square was a magnet. Maybe it had been calling my name as I crossed the Kansas border. Russ'

IGA Fine Foods, the quintessential small town grocery store if ever there was one. Like the Platonic fucking form of a small-town grocery store.

Now the real truth is I have a hobby–no, a fetish because it feels orgasmic when I make a find. It's like this. Real chefs, people who love food and don't just call it a paycheck, people who are artists of a sort, have an emotional connection to the ingredients. We look at catalogs and websites and anywhere we can find our working tools. Like grocery stores. We love grocery stores and markets of all kinds, any place and any ethnicity. Often the grubbiness of the store connotes a certain authenticity. The dirtier the better.

On my rare days off, I often walk the city without purpose, just to get out of the claustrophobic professional kitchen and my own cramped apartment. And I always hear the siren call of grocery stores. Bodegas, ethnic places all over the five boroughs, even the new Whole Foods in Brooklyn or on Columbus Circle. Bazaars, pop-ups, open-air markets. Size and shape and smell don't matter. Have you ever experienced rose water from a Halal grocery? Or real curry powder, not that jacked-up processed shit you get at Wal-Mart? Or fresh pasta from a pop-up in Little Italy from a couple that doesn't speak a word of English but clearly is as geeked out by the fresh semonlina as you are and you speak the same language of food? That's my church, my sermon, my joy.

So I went in. Maybe I would even meet the eponymous "Russ". "Morning!" It was a balding fifty-ish man with a green apron, organizing what few shopping carts the store offered. "Need one of these?"

"No thanks. Just browsing. Might get a couple of things for dinner but don't know what that might be."

"Sounds good. Let me know if you're looking for anything special. We got the usual on sale as the signs out front say but we got in a case of hummus yesterday. You look like a hummus man. Seems to be going fast." Balding man moved on to tend to his work. Hummus? Fucking hummus in Kiowa, Kansas?

I wandered to the right, always the home of produce and fruits. Meat in the back, dairy to the left. Sauces begin on the right, snacks and drinks and processed shit in the middle, butt-wipe and paper towels, foil and zipper lock bags, frozen foods, and maybe a bakery as you finally get to the milk, cheese and eggs. It's grocery store destiny. But it's the little things in between that make the difference, the small gems of region or demographics or trend that light up my world. I wondered what's in the middle of fucking nowhere beside hummus.

"I'm sorry!" A female voice interrupted my judgmental reverie. I turned around.

"Beth?"

I didn't expect to see her. But maybe I wanted to. Maybe I needed to.

11

BETH

Jack seemed out of place. And yet he seemed to be in the right place, somehow. He was clearly surprised to find me and only after an awkward silence and a few moments staring at each other was he able to let forth some kind of greeting.

"Hey there." He was trying to form a coherent sentence. It seemed up to me to offer some form of grace.

"It's good to see you again." My opening salvo.

"Good to see you too." He answered, then went silent, not quite knowing how to continue.

"You doing ok?" Another simple question, but more silence followed. I looked down at his clenched hands holding tight to a basket that was empty.

"No, not really. Jill and I had a fight this morning over what comes next. I live in New York and she seems unwilling to move there with me."

"Unwilling or unable? Should she move there at all?" As soon as I said it I regretted my move. It was a philosopher's habit of searching for clarity. My few friends call it going for the jugular but I prefer direct conversation rather than platitudes. I saw a flash of irritation in Jack.

"Yeah. She should go. She can't live by herself."

"That's not what I asked." Another move for the jugular. "I didn't ask whether you think she should go, but whether New York and moving would be right for her. This difference is in value. Would the move be for her or for you?"

"Why shouldn't she go?" I could see his hands grip the basket even tighter.

"Because this is her home. I know she has agoraphobia ,so it's not just some simple attitudinal shift she needs to make. These are her surroundings, her four walls, her familiarity and her identity. You take her out of that, you crush her. Hell, I don't even know her, but I think I see that."

"OK, granted, but how does that occur? I can't move here. MY identity is in New York, those are my four fucking walls."

"Bullshit. I bet you hate New York. You think you can be New York because you act New York and talk New York. You even swear New York and then claim it's you. But it's not. You are a farm kid from Oklahoma. You're in another place right now but you've also lived in a lot of places. Were you a hippie environmentalist when you lived in Portland?"

"You knew I lived in Portland? And I don't hate New York." He sat the basket on the floor and turned back to me.

"Guilty. I kept up, through my dad. I'm just saying that living in New York does not make you. Also, moving does not break you. Sorry, didn't mean to sound like a one-liner psychobabble quip. You get what I mean, right?"

He knew exactly what I meant. He turned away for a moment, staring at the Ragu. When he turned back, he sighed deeply for a moment, collecting himself.

"I do understand…but I need to think on it. The truth is, I'm pissed, and I need to clear my head to get straight and figure out a solution. Enough on that for now. Cool?"

I nodded in agreement. There was that awkward silence again.

We both began. "What are you shopping for?"

'What's going on for dinner?" It all blended together but it broke the tension.

He took the lead. "So, what are you shopping for, dinner? Couldn't help but notice what was in your cart. Looks like a quick spaghetti thing?" He pointed to the dried pasta and jarred sauce.

"Yeah, with all the stuff of the last few days, Dad didn't have anything for dinner. I said I would go out and grab something small and maybe we could do a bigger shopping tomorrow. Nothing fancy here, kind of a poor-girl- in-grad school kind of dinner. I was even going to get a bad red wine to go along. Fancy indeed!"

"Can I make a suggestion, maybe take up your grad school redux to something a little more palatable? I don't want to intrude but I think jarred sauce sucks." He caught himself. "Sorry, that was pretty judgey. I like food, good food, you know?"

I laughed. "Yeah, I know. It's kind of what you do for a living. I'm game. Kick it up a notch."

"You ever had arrabbiatta?"

"That's the hot one, right? I was in Italy for a while, research, writing, ok just academic playing on someone else's dime."

"That's right! Look, it's really easy. Put the sauce back. Grab two cans of tomatoes. You have olive oil? Garlic? Red pepper flakes?"

"I know Dad doesn't have any of that. He's meat and potatoes."

He looked stumped. He probably couldn't fathom not having those things around all the time–olive oil, vinegar, onions, spices, all of it all the time. It was like having toilet paper. You never ran out and you never went without.

"You have a pen and paper? I can write down your list and the instructions. See, you chop the garlic and then put it and the red pepper flakes in hot olive oil, not too hot because the garlic will burn, and then when it's ready, you ..."

I cut him off. What the hell was I doing? Logic be damned. "I have a better idea. Why don't you come over to our place and cook this? We'll shop together then you get to cook and teach and write it down all at once. I'll even splurge for a better bottle of wine–maybe ten bucks instead of five!" Me, the big spender. But then, "Oh wait, Jill..."

He was caught off guard and took a moment to ponder. I wanted to say something, but he spoke first.

"Better idea. We shop together. You buy the ingredients. I buy the wine. Ten-dollar wine sucks. You either spend five and know you're getting shitty wine or you go big. I'll go big." Clearly, he was on more solid ground now that the conversation had turned from emotions to food and wine.

"You come over to our place. Bring your dad. I'll cook. Jill will help. She loves this recipe. It was one of the first things I taught her when she got into cooking. Well, not really taught her. I told her about it over the phone and she made it. Actually, she made it for an entire week until Mom told her to stop. I bet she hasn't made it since then."

He stopped then and his excitement seemed to soften.

"It will be a way for Jill and I to say thank you for all you've done. Won't do it justice, but food is the best gift I can give you."

"I think that would be the best gift I've had in a long time." And I meant it. We gathered our ingredients and checked out.

"I'm over there." He pointed at his car across the square. "Seven-ish?"

"Sounds good. I'll see you then." I turned to go to my car but hesitated "Hey Jack–I think Jill is pretty cool. I thought you should know." He mumbled a small thanks but by that time I was moving to my car. It's good to catch people by surprise.

I almost missed the first turn onto the dirt roads as I crossed the border to drive back to Ray's. It was unfamiliar but I was also lost in thoughts. Why was I intrigued by Jack? I mean, I get it, he was someone from a long time ago and our situations had put us together, but why him? He was abrasive, cocky, kind of a jerk. But he also had something else, something in the way he cared about Jill, about food. He was different from the other guys in my life.

We approached Jack's place and I made a quick decision. Instead of continuing to Ray's I turned in the drive waiting for Jack to follow me up to the front door. I could see Jack's confusion as I got out.

"I thought you were headed back to your place. You didn't need to stop."

"I know," I agreed. "But I thought I might stop in and check on Jill. I mean, I know you got this, but I wanted to see how she was doing. You said you left pissed."

Jack immediately smiled. "I think that's a grand idea."

Jill was sitting on the couch watching the Food Channel and vigorously taking notes. She looked up with a smile, "Hey you two!".

It was as if it was perfectly normal for us to appear together.

"I just stopped in to see if you were doing ok. Jack and I ran into each other at the store in town and he said you were upset when he left." I glanced at Jack.

Jack took the cue. "Yeah, I told Beth we had been talking about what to do after the funeral with me in New York and you here. I'm sorry. I didn't mean to make you mad or sad or anything. I was angry and I didn't deal with it very well. My bad. Seems like you're ok?"

Jill looked up from the TV.

"I've seen this one before. I already know that recipe. When will they put something new on? Re-runs suck. Oops, sorry. Mom says ..." she paused. "Mom *used to* say I couldn't say that word."

"Totally ok with me to say it."

That seemed to put Jill at ease.

"Yeah, I'm kind of mad but not really. I mean, Mom is gone and everything and that makes me sad. But I don't want to leave here. I can't leave here. I won't leave here."

"I get it," I said. "That would make me mad and sad, too." I looked over at Jack, who was silent. "Jack?"

He paused for a second, looked at me and mouthed a silent thank you.

"Jill, we won't make you go. This is your home and you shouldn't be forced to go away. We'll just need to figure out how to make it all work. Not today, not right now, do we need to solve it, but we will. Actually, we can have a longer conversation tonight, all of us. Beth and Ray are coming back for dinner. And I'm making fucking arrabbiatta!"

He said it with emphasis and joy because he knew it would delight his sister. And it did. More than any TV show, more than anything else he could have said, announcing that he was making hot spicy pasta and that Ray and I would be along for the ride, well, that changed everything.

12

JILL

Oh. My. God.

Beth is coming over for dinner. I am like freaking out. I want everything to be perfect. I'll have to get the perfect table settings and maybe some candles because candles set the mood. I don't know where Mom put the extras. I saw the best candles on Martha Stewart's show and they were exquisite I tell you.

Martha Stewart went to prison, you know. At first I thought it might be for murder or something crazy. But then I was watching Entertainment Weekly and they made a big deal out of it in the promos but all she did was fraud. Measly old fraud. That's a fraud I tell you! Making like it was murder and then just letting us viewers down big time. I wonder if she did table settings from prison or even in prison 'cause I bet that place was really cold and really drab and could have used some pepping up! Candles and Martha Stewart would do the trick for sure.

I made Mom go get me some candles when we ran out. It was at Whole Food and they were cool and all, purple with pink swirly things at the bottom, but they weren't elegant like Martha

Stewart's. I told Mom this just wouldn't do and then she yelled at me and I cried and went up to my room. I stayed there for three whole days until Mom said she would go to the Home Goods store the next time she went to the city and that she would find me some Martha Stewart candles. And she did! It was *tres eleganto,* indeed. We dined by candlelight all that week. I think that's the last time we used candles and that was like five years ago. So I wonder where the extras are. We have to have candles tonight for Beth.

We will have to get the good china out of the hutch in the hallway. We used it the same week as the candles and even a few times after that. Mom liked to use it. She said it reminded her of good times and family, whatever that means. She told me it had been her mom's and before that her mema's, who had brought it over from Europe when she came to live in Oklahoma. She said I could have it when she's gone so I guess it's mine now.

Who will get it after me?

13

JACK

Beth and Ray arrived precisely at 7pm. My guess was this wasn't Beth as much as it was Ray, the farmer's predilection to be exact. Ray was dressed in his typical jeans and button-down shirt, not his everyday farming shirt and not quite his Sunday-church shirt, but something in between, like what he would wear if he was headed out to the movies.

Beth, on the other hand, appeared to have paid particular attention to her dress. Or was it just me? I wasn't sure what to expect. It was just dinner and maybe, I thought jeans and a blouse would be the thing, sort of a copy of if not an exact replica of what was in the grocery store. Maybe I was expecting some Betty Friedan feminist shit that expressed her complete rejection of men and dating. Her outfit would scream, "Not for you anytime, anywhere, Mr. Man."

But her impression was spectacular in a beautiful sundress. And somehow that also didn't fit with my expectation of a philosophy professor. I came to a quick realization that I was being an asshole.

"Can I get you both a drink?" I pointed at the beautiful table Jill had put out. Nice tablecloth, the bottle of red wine we had bought earlier, plates and silverware laid precisely, napkins bound by a ring on top of the plate. To the left was a separate platter with some small nibbles of meat and cheese as well as cheese straws.

I could see Beth's amazement at the set-up.

"Yeah, Jill went to town. It's the food channel come to life. Pretty cool, huh?"

Jill burst in right at that moment. "Hi guys! How are you?" "Jill, this is amazing!" Beth was authentic in her praise. I could see Jill stand a little taller.

"Thanks. I've wanted to do something like this, like, for forever. But we really didn't have people over when Mom was around. I had it all lined up in my head, though. I even did the charcuterie and made the cheese straws."

"So, you still need that drink?" I inquired. I plucked a beer from the fridge for Ray and poured glasses of wine for Beth and me. I had pasta water on a simmer, so I invited everyone to the table, libations and nibbles at hand. Jill was giddy.

"You get any more information on the funeral?" Ray asked.

"Looks like it will be on Thursday. Small memorial, graveside burial. Seems like Mom didn't have a lot of close friends. What happened? She used to be real involved with her church groups and with folks up in town, but there's not a lot of that anymore. I called the church and the secretary knew who she was but the pastor didn't."

"Yep, your Mom kind of turned inward these last few years. She wasn't prone to get out much except to do the regular shopping or head to the doctors. Didn't seem to get much joy out of people really. You know, I'd come check on her every couple of days, see if she or Jill didn't need something. Funny, but the conversations got shorter this last year, like she was fixin' to prepare for going away."

Ray was never the poet, but he had always had a good sense of people and the world.

Jill chimed in as well. "Yeah, Mom didn't talk to me much either. I just mostly watched TV or was in my room. Aren't these cheese straws the best?"

I reached over to Jill and took her hand. "I would totally sell these in my restaurant!"

I glanced over at Beth, consciously looking for approval. I wanted to impress her. She gave a slight nod at me, like she knew exactly that this was what Jill needed in that moment, that she didn't want to talk about her mother being gone and she needed to be reaffirmed in her cooking and in her being.

Our table conversation moved to some of the usual topics at any farm kitchen, the weather, the crops, an update on people in town. After a few minutes, I got up to cook the main meal. Jill got up to help but I gently asked, "Hey, Jill...do you mind if Beth helps me out? I promised I would teach her this dish. She tells me she can't cook!"

"I did not say that!" Beth said it loudly but with a sheepish grin on her face. "What I said was that I tend to cook quick and when you're cooking for one person, you don't do gourmet."

"That's a terrible excuse! Come on. Jill, will you chop the garlic? Beth, want to come work with me on the rest of the sauce? Ray, feel free to turn on the ballgame if you want."

"No, I'll stick around and watch. Game doesn't start 'til late. Cards against the Angels in Anaheim."

Jill went to the cutting board to chop garlic as well as some of the Kalamata olives I had set out. At the stove, I reached for a large sauté pan, put it on the burner and then turned up the heat to get the water boiling. "Get a big pan. You want space for things to move around. Heat the pan before you put anything else in. By the time the pan is hot, the water for the pasta should be at a robust boil."

My audience watched the pan get hot and the water start to roll. Even Ray seemed to have taken on the role of student. Jill chimed in with color commentary. "He's pretty good isn't he?" She was recognizing the teacher and master in the room. "He taught me a lot, even over the phone!"

The pan smoke and the steam from the boiling water hovered above the stove. "See that cloud? It means we're ready. It's all going to happen quick now. Jill, you ready?"

"I am!" Pilot and co-pilot together. Beth was amazed.

The pasta went in and I filled the sauté pan with lots of olive oil. It immediately began to bubble and splatter in the hot pan.

"Why so much?"

"For this dish, the oil is the basis of the sauce. It's not just to fry up the other things, but it gives the dish substance and life." Next came the garlic and olives along with salt and pepper, both in small bowls to the side of the oven.

"And now two key ingredients." The teacher was telling everyone to pay attention.

"See the garlic, how it's getting a little brown at the edges? If it gets too brown, it's ruined, but it needs some color just like this. Take the pan off the direct heat and here's where you toss in the chilis and the capers with brine." I pointed at a spice jar of dried red chile as well as an opened jar of tiny green berries.

I took the top off the spice and poured in a generous amount of chili.

"How much do you put in? Seems like a lot." Beth was focused intently on the lesson.

"It's as much as you need." I caught myself. I don't teach cooking often but when I do it's with colleagues, other chefs, not newbies. I needed to be more precise. "It's probably a tablespoon at least. You need more than you think because the sauté will take out some of the heat and so will the sauce itself. I tend to like mine hot. But test it. You like more heat, you put in more, you like less, put in less. It's beautiful chemistry!"

I was loving this, the food, the company, the teaching. I sensed Beth could feel my exhilaration.

"When you've sautéed the chili for maybe thirty seconds off heat, put the pan back on the burner and then add a couple of spoonfuls of capers. Then pour in the brine from the jar. That's the trick. The capers add some bite along with olives, but the brine gives it this silky quality, a little rustic, a little funky. Some people like anchovies for the funk and silk but I dig the capers and brine. Let that all go and start to combine for a minute."

The pan was bubbling and through the steam all the ingredients were beginning to combine, a synthesized and elegant dish from what were once individual ingredients.

"I see it. It's coming together, isn't it?"

"Yep ... and when it starts to look pretty thick, almost glossy, then add your tomatoes."

I reached over for two opened cans of tomatoes.

"These are basic and will do the trick. There's a specialty can of San Marzano's that I can get in New York or I'll do fresh tomatoes in season. But in the absence, just a can or two of Hunt's are perfect. No more, no less."

"Next trick ... bring it to a quick boil. Well, not really a boil, but bring the temperature up to where it's starting to sputter. Then turn it down so it's a gentle simmer. You want to do that for about five minutes. Then turn it off and cover it. Let it sit while we get the pasta ready." Everything happened quickly then. The sauce got covered, I drained the pasta, topped it with more olive oil, then uncovered the sauce to add the pasta to the sauté pan a little at a time until all of it was incorporated. I added some reserved pasta water at the end.

"Another trick?" Beth directed at me.

"Oh yeah, I guess so. I always do it, so I guess I don't think of it as a trick. But the pasta water gives it more shape. It binds it all together. The Italians do this with every pasta dish. Why doubt the experts?"

And so it was done. I put the pasta into the serving bowl, pulled out a loaf of Italian bread from the oven and brought both to the table. I filled glasses of wine for everyone- even Ray–and we sat down to the meal.

Ray asked, "Are we saying grace?"

Jill chimed in, "I will!" And before anyone could say anything, she began.

We all held hands.

"Dear God. Bless this house and this home. Bless the people here with us and those not with us. Bless this food before us and the food that goes to nourish others. Especially bless my mom in heaven who is with you now. Amen."

Beth squeezed my hand. I squeezed back. We let go and began to eat. After a couple of bites in silence, Beth spoke.

"Ok, look, this is easily the best pasta I have ever had. I was in Italy for a couple of days and had pasta there and it was incredible. But truly, this is better." She was looking directly at me.

"Well, thanks, I guess. It is pretty good, but I've never been to Italy and I don't eat out much. I picked it up from some other chefs over the years, a little technique here and there when we were cooking staff meals. I mean, those staff meals are probably the best meals I've ever had in my life."

Beth asked, "Staff meals? What's a staff meal?"

Jill intervened. "I know! It's the meal that gets cooked by the staff before the dinner service or whatever service starts. Sometimes it's what's on the menu but sometimes it's whatever the chef wants to cook for everyone. Right Jack? I know 'cause he told me and then I saw it on TV one time. There was this one meal where a chef did like three courses for the staff with only mushrooms and cheese!"

"That's it. I don't think I've ever had the mushroom and cheese menu for a staff meal, but I've gotten everything from A to Z and sometimes I've cooked alongside them. Actually, this arrabbiata is my go-to for a staff meal. Seems to be a hit most times."

"Why's the food so good at staff meals?"

I paused. "Two things, I think. It's because the cook is getting to create what he or she wants. It's not on the menu, there's no rules, it's just putting out great food with the ingredients you want. The second thing is with that freedom comes more emotion and more intention, maybe more attention as well. It's the very essence of what we're doing. And as a chef, you don't get to do that very often."

There was silence. I wondered if I had shaken the moment, too profound for the joys we had found in eating together. Beth looked at me and started to open her mouth but Jill beat her to it.

"That is so freaking cool!"

Dinner ended. Everyone sat back, satisfied. The meal had been perfect. Food, conversation, wine. It was memorable. The silence that enveloped the table wasn't uncomfortable, instead, it sat softly. In almost a whisper, Jill said "I'll clean up." The cleaning up part wasn't odd for Jill, it was the whisper that got my attention.

"You good?"

"I am. I'm just a little sad that it all has to be over. It was so cool. And I want the arrabiata again."

"Well maybe tonight is over but we can do this again." Like a child, Jill pounced on the idea.

"When? Tomorrow?"

"Maybe, just maybe." I said it dismissively because I knew tonight would be hard to recreate. It was the great chefs who had somehow mastered the ability to do this night after night for patrons. The silence that followed was uncomfortable. I could feel Jill moving inward, physically retracting herself away from the table and me because of my words.

This time Ray intervened.

"Jill honey. Why don't you and I clean up together?"

They both moved away to the sink leaving me alone with Beth for the first time since the grocery store.

"I feel for you. That's hard." Beth could sense my struggle.

"Yeah, it always keeps coming back. Fuck!" I said it under my breath, exasperated. But then I looked up at Beth and saw authentic concern. "Sorry. The swearing's kind of a habit."

"No apologies. Seems to make sense to me. Jill wants company, she needs to be taken care of. She can't leave because of her agoraphobia and you are the next best thing now that your mom is gone." She paused. "Sorry, that was kind of harsh. It's the philosopher in me to remove the emotion and state

104

observations. Yes, it's hard and I can't imagine what kind of place that puts you in." In the span of those few words, I knew I had found a friend, someone as deep as Derek, a confidant. She said it was ok to swear, to be angry, and had identified the issue right away without judgment. Isn't that what you need in a friend?

"Do you want to go take a walk around the farm? I used to do it every night as a kid, about this time before the sun went down. It was my ritual. A way to get my headspace clear, maybe a way to get out of what felt like being trapped in a cell. If I could get out, then maybe I wasn't like Jill and Mom."

"I truly don't want to intrude. But if the offer is there and real, I'd love to go."

I smiled.

14

BETH

We exited out the side door right off the kitchen and turned towards the pasture and the barn. I thought that was where we were headed until he stopped in front of a dilapidated structure sagging under the weight of its own age. The wood boards that framed the entire building were worn, most frayed at the edges, some already in pieces and broken. I had some memory of this place but I couldn't locate the when and why.

"This was my arena!" Jack spread his arms wide as if announcing this to me and to the world at large.

I looked again at the structure and could see a basketball hoop hanging - barely - to the building. Memories were starting to return, me trying to dribble a ball or loft it into the hoop. It was fuzzy.

"I would come out here for hours and shoot. When I was pissed I would shoot. When I was happy, I would shoot. I'd make up these games, Celtics versus Lakers, Bird versus Magic. I'd set a clock with quarters and everything."

I held up my hands in dismay. "I have no idea what you are

talking about. I get the whole put the basketball in the hoop thing but why would some aviary creature be involved with magic and money?"

It took a second for Jack to translate my confusion. But when he did, he let out a cackle.

"That is fucking awesome. I love that you have no idea what I am talking about. Those were two great NBA players - Larry Bird and Magic Johnson - and quarters are the segments of a game. And yes, I'm mansplaining!"

Then I cackled. "I love that you know mansplaining. Don't do it again."

He took me around the side of the building, down a worn pathway and finally to the backside where the remnants of a door sat open to what was the basement, almost a cave-like room given the lack of walls. "Jack, wait. I have some memory of this. Have we been here before?"

"I don't know. Probably. This was the chicken coop. It was also my place to hide when I didn't want to be found. It was my job to clean it and get the eggs so no one else came by. It was my own space, even more so when we quit chickens when I was about eleven or twelve. See, look there."

He pointed to a couple of rusty nails attached to the standards in the coop. I looked closely and could see a scrap of paper, maybe two inches by two inches, hanging from one of the nails.

"What is it?"

"That's what's left of my baseball card collection. I nailed cards all over this place. It was like the fucking Met in the City, only instead of Matisse I had Mike Schmidt and George Brett."

"Again, I have no idea who those people are. I do know baseball cards though." Jack laughed again.

"Yeah, I had them everywhere in here. When I left after high school, I tore them all down and took them with me. Cheap psychology, but I wanted to take some piece of the farm with me and I didn't want Mom or Jill having anything of mine. I ended up throwing all of the cards away the next year. Somehow it felt immature and young when I was out on my own to keep baseball cards when I was a real adult in the real cooking world. Kind of stupid really."

"No, not really. I think we always discard the old in favor of the new. When we're reinventing ourselves we have to get rid of the things that remind us of the past. Natural I think. I've done it a few times."

"You have?"

"Sure." Jack didn't ask any further. It was like he knew I had done it and I didn't need to give him examples.

We moved out of the chicken coop and further down the worn path to the creek.

He took my hand. "It gets a little rocky here and we need to get up the other side of the creek bank."

"Are you mansplaining again?"

"Nope, I promise! Just trying to help."

"Well in that case, offer accepted." I liked his hand in mine.

We moved up the creek bank and came to the fence that defined the pasture.

"Here, there's an opening."

Jack picked up a stake in the fence, peeling back the wire. He pulled it past him and left a small opening that was easy enough for a single person to slide through.

"Kind of cool that it's still here. I made this when I was a kid, a way for me to get past the chicken coop over there to the barn. It felt ..." He paused. "Sneaky. I could be the stealth ninja agent through the fields and not have to deal with my wacko mother and batshit sister."

He replaced the fence after we got through and pointed out a dim path in the woods. I could see a clearing on the other side, and as we got further along, I spotted train tracks just past where the trees ended.

Jack read my mind as I wondered why we were here. "It's always been a natural barrier for cattle when they were here. Our land ends at the tracks and cows don't want to get stuck. Almost like a cattle guard. Come on. I want to show you something and see if it's there."

We walked to the tracks, moving up to the north about a hundred yards. Jack looked around trying to find a marker out in the fields to fix his position.

"Yep, should be about here." He peered into the space between the tracks, made harder by the diminishing sunlight and kicked around the rocks. Suddenly spying what he was after, he bent down and picked something up. In his hand I could see a thin brown oblong object.

"Know what this is?"

"I hope it's not a dried-out turd!"

"It's a penny. It's one of my wish pennies. Look!" Jack pointed out a scattering of similar objects all along one side of the tracks. They weren't in piles but instead were distributed amongst the rocks. They covered three or four square feet and my quick scan suggested there were fifty or more.

"I would come up here, just like we did. Mostly it was when I was pissed. I would take a penny and leave it on the track and make a wish. Usually, it was a wish to get the hell out of here. Sometimes a wish about a girl or maybe finding a million dollars, but the wish I had the most was to leave. I'd come back the next day to see if the penny was still there, flattened out or if it had been tossed aside by the train. If it was flat and still on the track, the wish would come true. If not, the wish was discarded. Train karma."

"And did the pennies stay? I assume so since your wish seemed to come true."

"See all those? Those are the wishes that came true. I'd come back the next day to see where the penny landed. If it was on the track, I kept it here, right where you see it. If not, I threw it into the pasture. I'll tell you there are a lot more pennies scattered somewhere out in the field."

I picked up one of the pennies. It was smooth, all traces of etching and writing removed by the weight and friction of the train. I had to ask.

"Did you ever make a wish about me?" He looked away sheepishly with a grin, like he didn't want to answer the question. I also saw him mumble something under his breath that rhymed with duck. I laughed and released him from his embarrassment. "What was that you just said? I couldn't hear you?" He laughed while he turned back around to me. "Can you make another wish on this one? Like in your karmic interpretation of the universe, can I take this one and double down?"

"No way!" Jack was emphatic. "One penny, one wish. That's the way it goes."

"You have any pennies on you?"

"Seems I just might." Jack reached into his pants and pulled out a handful of change from which he plucked two pennies. He handed one to me.

"So how do you do this?"

"Hold it tight in your hand, really tight. Hold your hand in front and then in your mind, you say a wish. Don't say it out loud.

If you do, then it won't come true. Then put it on the tracks. Just that simple."

I clutched the penny and held out my hand towards Jack. I closed her eyes and wished. And wished some more. I put the penny on the track.

"What did you wish?"

"Am I supposed to tell you? Can I?"

"Well, the universe would think it's ok if you tell me."

"Maybe later. I'm going to keep that one close for now. How about you? Are you going to make a wish?"

"Nah, my wishes came true when I got out of here. Don't want to fuck with the universe when they've granted my very deepest request. You only get so much, you know?"

"Why's that?"

"Well, my theory is that we get granted a certain kind of life. We ask for it at an early stage, the universe says yes, and then we move down that path. We get challenged, we get off course, but essentially we stay on the same path. We can't ask for more than we're given."

"Isn't that a bit cynical, like you can't change your life or you can't have a second chance?"

"I don't know. Maybe."

We let the silence sit, and this time it was more uncomfortable. I didn't know how to address his cynicism and Jack could see I was pressing. Whatever spark had happened with the pennies, had disappeared. For now.

"Come on. There's one more thing I want to show you." He seemed excited again, his face and voice asking me to come along to the next memory.

He took us to another dim path back through the treeline. I could tell we were angling back to the house. By now it was getting dark, fragments of sun peeking through the trees. After a bit, Jack stopped and pointed at a large shadow in front of us. What stood before me was the back end of the barn, or at least I thought it was the barn. I had obviously seen it from the front as a kid and more recently as we made our way to the chicken coop. But here the back end was less defined, a colorless wall in the fading light with the classic barn truss and roof to provide hazy definition. At the top there was a square opening and I could almost make out a two-paneled door at the bottom.

As we got closer, I could see that weather and time had dulled the barn similar to the chicken coop and in some places the paint had worn off completely, showing dilapidated and damaged wood. It was an indication of a farm that had seen better days, a time when it was lived in and cared for.

Jack pointed to the door. "Here, I want to take you to the second floor."

The creaking of the doors filled the silence of the night.

We moved through to a small staircase on the left and ascended. I noticed a tang in the air, something fetid and rotting, like sunlight hadn't gotten in this space for a long time. The dirt and critters had it all to themselves.

Jack stopped at the top step and motioned for me to join him. When I did, I saw a vast second floor spread out across the entire structure. There were remnants of hay stashed across the space, two stray bales as well, but otherwise empty. At the far end towards the direction of the house was another opening, this one far larger than the one I had initially seen out back. The last glimmers of an Oklahoma sunset shone through that opening and it cast a warm glow of orange light upon the entire scene. My mom always called this "country pretty". It was the only scant praise she could find for Oklahoma and seemed to come straight out of Country Living.

"Is that what you wanted me to see?" I pointed to the sunset letting Jack know I thought this was great.

"Kind of, but not really. I mean, this is goddamn beautiful and I'd be lying if I said I knew it was here." He was sheepish again. It was endearing.

"Then what? You wanted to get me up here to steal a kiss and hope that was my wish? Is that a long-lost penny in your hand?"

He laughed at me. "Not a bad idea either. But no. Look up there?"

He pointed towards the far end, right above the opening where the sun was setting. The angle of the sun made it hard to see anything. But above it I could see a perch. The indirect light kept things in shadow but I could make out two objects on the perch.

"See it?"

"On the perch there?"

Jack emitted a soft sound then, not quite a loud screech, but a guttural murmuring at the top range of his masculine voice. "Whoooooo ... whooooooo ...."

The two objects came to life as both owls turned their heads to look for the source of the sound. Their faces were a lighter shade, a white against brown feathering. Even in the dim light I could make out the big owl eyes, expressive and peering at us. After a moment, one swooped away, right at us but then angling in the direction of the smaller opening at the end of the barn. The other followed and soon they had both disappeared into the gloaming.

"Did we scare them?"

"A little probably. But they would have left soon anyway. This is the time to hunt."

"How did you know?"

"I didn't. I was hoping they would be here. As a kid, this was my other hiding place. I would come up here pretty much every day. I loved the way I was above everything, that I could look down on the world and spy on things."

"That's a little creepy!"

"Maybe it's the stalker in me!" Jack was laughing, maybe at me, perhaps at himself. Still endearing. "But those two owls were here. They were always here. It didn't matter what season, the temperature, anything. They would be here in the morning and leave at night. And they didn't miss a day. I went to the library to figure it out and the book told me that owls have mates for life. They live in pairs and establish their house, their place, their territory. Once established, they don't leave and they'll fight other owls for that supremacy. They also live for a long time. You know, wise old owl? So here they are twenty years later since I saw them."

I sat looking at him. "So you haven't seen them in twenty years? And you took me up here, hoping?"

"Fucking cool, huh? I mean, I stopped in, maybe, ten years ago on the way back from Portland to New York and they were still here. But yeah, I didn't know."

"Why did you want to show me?"

He didn't answer. In our time as kids he had never told me about the owls and never took me to the barn. He turned and went down the stairs quietly. I followed him in silence. In the near distance, we could see the lights from the kitchen and the living room. At the gate, Jack paused and looked back to the barn.

"I think those owls are one of the great things about this place. I have a lot of bad memories here, but I also like to think that things can be better or more pleasant or more something because of the owls. They see it and love it, even with all the crap. I wanted to show you that piece of goodness here. I wanted to see it myself."

This time I reached out and took his hand. "Thank you. Truly, thank you."

Jack looked embarrassed and hastily changed the subject.

"So, what did you wish for?"

"What?" I was confused and didn't pick up on the context of his question.

"Your wishing penny. What did you wish for?"

"That I get to stay here."

"Why would you want to stay here?"

"Because …" I paused. "Maybe we'll talk about it later."

15

JILL

Dinner was really great last night. Beth and Ray came over and we had arrabiata that Jack made. It was soooooo good! Jack is the best cook. I think I will make him dinner tonight. Maybe a casserole. There's been these really good casseroles on Pioneer Woman lately. She is so good and she lives on a ranch, kind of like me. Maybe something with noodles and burger. I don't know yet. I'll have to think about it. Jack will need to get me some ingredients, so I better tell him about it today.

Jack and Beth went out walking and while they did, me and Ray cleaned up. He's great. He's always been a good friend for me and for my mom. He asked me what I was thinking about doing now that Mom had died. I said I really didn't know. I'm getting better with that question, especially if someone asks it more like Ray than like Jack.

Jack gets all mad like he wants a perfect answer. Ray asked me real gentle. And when I said I didn't know, he didn't press me. He only said that he would help in any way he could. He even said I could come live with him but that won't work because I have never been to his house and I really can't leave.

Well, I kind of remember going to his house one time as a kid when his wife Ruth was there. It wasn't a scary place at all. He was nice to me and let me go play in his basement where there were all these books and paintings and old rocks. It kind of smelled funny down there but it was a place all my own. Ruth brought me some cookies and soda too. I was fine for a while but then started to have "an episode". "Episode" is what Mom called my freak-outs.

I just get scared if I'm not here at home. But it's more than scared. It really feels like I am about to die, even though I don't really know what that's like to die. I can't breathe and I scream and I feel like someone is holding me down and in place and I can't even move. I get real bad pains in my arms and legs. At least that's how I remember it.

I haven't been out for maybe almost sixteen years. I'm forty-two right now, so it would have been when I was twenty-six. Mom had this great idea to have me in therapy all through high school and then in my twenties. Some guy would come around the house and talk to me. We talked about my anxiety a lot! He wanted me to take a step towards the door and just be ok with it. I did one time and started screaming like a banshee. But he kept asking and I kept trying. We didn't get anywhere.

He even tried hypnosis. I loved it because it was like the best sleep ever. He even made me do things like touch my nose and my arms and one time even made me pretend to hold a baseball bat in my hands even when there wasn't one there. They took a video to show me. I was so silly!

But then he did a different kind of hypnosis and said we were going to go walk out the door, just around the dirt driveway. I remember that I could hear him doing this and that my body was moving that direction. But I didn't want to. And all the scared stuff happened to me. The breathing and the arms and the pain. I screamed really loud and opened my eyes. I was outside, two steps from the door is all but it could have been miles. I remember the doctor picked me up off the ground and took me back in. I stayed in my room and my bed for two whole weeks. That doctor never returned. No doctor ever returned. I got happy again.

So I don't know what I'm gonna do. I hope Jack will come live with me but I don't think he likes it much here. Maybe I could have Beth convince him. She is so cool. Or maybe we could find another friend to come live here with me. I don't think I can live on my own because I need a lot of things. And who would be here if I got hurt?

16

BETH

I woke up this morning and my first thought was of my wishing penny. I wanted to go back and see if it had been scattered or kept on the tracks. Would my wish come true or not? I really do want to stay here. Ohio isn't for me and Ray is getting older. I like the simplicity of things. No, it's not really that. I like the simplicity of the people. That's not condescending because the simplicity of the people is their actual power. There's no clamor for status or some move to impress you. That's been a constant at my college and all through graduate school. Who could you impress that day? Your colleague? Your thesis advisor? The other professors in the English department? You could even do it by shitting on some staff member by letting them know he or she didn't really count. What mattered most was the professors. No, people here are simple. There is no worry about impressions. Sure, people want to look nice and be nice and make sure others are happy. But at the core, there is a presentation of "this is who I am, take it or leave it."

The other thing I love is the simplicity of words. A conversation is small, but says so much. You don't have to dance around and add all kinds of language.

Yes, professors love their language. It's a way of showing off. But people here, well, people here get to the heart of the matter quickly. You either like a thing or you don't. You don't need to spend hours talking about the thing. There are no lectures in these flyover states.

I think Jack at his heart is one of these people. He doesn't like the b.s. of people either. It just comes out as anger more than anything. I bet that's a product of living in New York City. You have to constantly be on your guard, protect your turf. He doesn't like airs and I bet there are all kinds of airs there. I like Jack. He's a good man, maybe better than any I've met in a while. Our walk last night reminded me that maybe in all this recreating of myself that I'm in the midst of, maybe, just maybe, I need to think about some new relationships as well. And Jill. What about Jill? Sweet as ever, but crippled by never being able to leave the house. It wore her mom down. I asked Ray about it last night after dinner as we were washing up.

"Dad, what was Wanda like these last couple of years?"

He dried two plates before he spoke.

"She got ..." and he dried one more before he said, "...tired. I think it all just wore her down. If you could have seen her even ten years ago you would have seen a different lady."

Ray put the towel down and continued.

"She had a bunch of friends, always doing something at the community center or at church, even with all she had going on with Jill. Jack leaving was hard and she always told me she just didn't know how to make that right. That wore on her for sure. But Jill just got more ... needy. I don't know. The way Wanda described it was that Jill realized she was going to be inside all the time and needed things to do and really needed Wanda to get all those things. She couldn't say no."

"Did she ever ask you for help?"

"Not in so many words. I went over every week just to check in and if I missed a week she would call up the next day and wonder where I was. I took that as needing some company besides Jill, a friend she didn't have to go see, someone she didn't have to explain anything to."

"That's being a great friend." I looked Ray right in the eye when I said it. He looked away. I didn't know if it was embarrassment or emotion. But he kept on.

"Yeah, I tried. One time she even mentioned taking her own life. I don't know if she was serious but when we got to talking further about it she said she didn't really mean it because she knew Jill would go before her. She just needed to wait it out. That all changed the last two years when she got her diagnosis."

"Her what?" It felt like Ray was revealing something he shouldn't have.

"Yeah, she was sick. I guess I didn't realize she was this far along."

"With what?"

"Heart stuff. We made quite a pair."

He picked up the towel and dried a couple more plates before he spoke up.

"I had a good talk with Jill last night. She knows there's a problem right now but she's convinced Jack will stay. When I asked her why she just gave me that Jill smile and said she just knew. I wish we could all be so certain about life."

So do I.

17

JACK

What a fucking mess. Even after a great dinner last night and my walk with Beth, I woke up this morning and remembered my shit heap of a situation. I don't want to be here and I don't know what to do about Jill. This was never part of the plan. It was Mom's job to deal with this shit and I never imagined it would get passed on to me. I mean, I should have thought about it, because Mom was going to die at some point but Oklahoma was there and far away and I could live my fucking life. Mom would figure out what to do. Not me. That wasn't my gig.

But maybe there's been some upside. I haven't been on a walk or a date or anything with a girl in a while. There was some freedom there last night with Beth. She's cool. I mean, she's got this great sense of being here and now, of just being settled. It made me more settled being with her. New York keeps me going and moving all the time. There's not much space to just be. It's the next thing and then the next thing. The girls are like that, too. Where are we going to dinner? What are we doing tomorrow? Pace, energy, activity. It sucks.

But things slowed down with Beth last night. It was a great

dinner. Just cooking, you know? I haven't really taught cooking in a while. Truth be told, if there's been anything around teaching, I just yell at the line cooks to get it fucking right. Is that teaching? Maybe. But last night was cool. It was nice to take it slow and show someone who doesn't know how to really cook. And that shit was awesome, really.

But the walk … It got a little weird when she asked me why I showed her the owls. I don't know. It's just something I wanted to show her. I had other girlfriends in high school and I never even showed them. I kept it my secret because it was the place I could retreat. But with Beth, I wanted her to see it. Maybe I'm older and don't need to hide anymore. Maybe it's all bullshit anyway.

I have no idea why she would want to stay here. Anywhere, even fucking Ohio, is better than this place. What's the point here? It's just land and fucking farmers. There's no culture and the grocery stores suck. But in a weird way, maybe it's getting away from somewhere that matters. She's getting away from Ohio just like I had to get away from here. But where do you go to? Where would I go if I needed to get away from the City?

I need to get over to Ray's today. I told him we would talk about the funeral but I'm also gonna see if he can help with this Jill thing. I've got to get back and I wonder if he might look after Jill, maybe even permanently. He seems to care about her and shit, he's not going anywhere. Maybe he could check in with her every day or maybe we could get a home caretaker, kind of like someone with bad health who has a live-in with them.

Now if I could Walter Mitty the shit out of this, maybe Mom passing away will be the thing to get Jill out of this house. Mom babied her and gave in. She's gone, God rest here soul, so maybe a little at a time, that home health person could kick her ass and make her come around to getting out of this house. A little psychology, a little tough love, then she gets better and can come with me to New York. Or maybe she goes on her own.

Who am I fucking kidding?

I hope Beth will be there. I might see if she wants to go get a drink tonight. Actually, I think I'll go see what happened to her wishing penny. Might even leave a new one on the tracks myself. You never know.

I decided to walk to Ray's. It's only a quarter mile down the road and I had made that walk many times as a kid, a way to kill the weekend or summer boredom when shooting baskets or tromping in the pastures didn't do it for me. I turned right out of the driveway and made my way to the shelter belt of trees. It was still there, a worn path from my younger days and one the deer had kept alive over the years.

It was cool and shielded from the sun. Even this early I could feel the creep of the ominous signs of an oppressive Oklahoma making itself known. I picked up on a familiar scent in the bramble of vines to the left. Ground gourds everywhere.

I once asked Mom about them and her response was vague, that someone had probably planted them for decoration or for some fucking interior design motif. She reasoned critters had likely stolen the gourds out of a garden and deposited them into the shelter belt. Seeds got spread, gourds sprouted up all over, and no one really cared as long as the trees kept growing to protect the houses from weather.

Man, those gourds smelled like shit, especially if you pick them up. I mean, I have dealt with some malodorous shit in my kitchen life – French cheese, months old, putrefied veggies, rancid fish, you name it – but these gourds might be the worst. Pick them up and the scent would stay on your hands until a good scrubbing got it off. Mom would yell at me when she smelled it on me. You couldn't hide the scent from her or anyone. But fuck it, I did it anyways no matter what she said or even sometime, because of what she had said. I'd pick them up and aim at the nearest tree, sometimes pretending it was a pass to a wide receiver in the end zone as time expired or lobbing a grenade at an enemy. So I had to try again. I picked one up, hurled it towards a tree and completely missed my target, a tall elm about twenty feet away. I nailed it the second time. Maybe I wasn't aging so badly. I wiped my hands on the grass hoping to diminish the scent. No dice. It was still there. Comforting and off-putting all at once.

I made my way back out to the road, picking up a rock or two and flung them off into the barren fields. The season's wheat was on the cusp of being cut and it really was beautiful in a rustic-country sort of way. It was also familiar and soothing to my agitated soul.

Ray's place sits at the crossroads of two dirt thoroughfares tucked into the northwest corner. To the north of the house and behind the equipment barns and Ray's rock shop - he is a hell of an amateur gemologist - is the beginning of another wheat field. The property stretches for two more sections. To the west is his shelter belt of trees but instead of gourds, this one was filled with old cars. A '65 Fairlane, a '59 Chevy, a truck from the 1940's. None of them ran of course but had been deposited in the shelter belt to stand the test of years of hot summers and cool winters. I spent a lot of hours there, in the cars, pretending to drive and go somewhere, anywhere, other than here. Escape was the common theme for me then. Maybe it was the theme for me now. I wondered if the cars were still there.

The house itself is modest, a single level, porches on the east and south looking directly at the roads, and a mottled white with brown trim. It needed a good painting, and the white was speckled with all the brown dirt, blown harsh from the fields until it ran into the house. His driveway and front door were on the west side, near the most immense garden that sat between the house and shelter belt. That garden produced a mighty bounty each year. Even when Ray's second wife, Ruth, passed away, Ray continued to work there for hours, weeding and watering, cutting and pruning, canning and tilling until the last bits wore out around Thanksgiving. Ray always said he needed a hobby when she died. The garden lasted from March until November and the rock shop for the months in between. Loneliness will make men busy, it seems.

I got to the front door and knocked. There were no doorbells out here. You knocked and yelled "hey" attempting to get someone's attention. If you knew them well, you might yell "hey" as you walked in. Life on the Plains was like that. Only strangers stood at the door waiting for someone to arrive. But I stayed put. I felt like a stranger.

Ray arrived and opened the door. He looked at me with a bemused smile. "Why didn't you just come on in?"

"Didn't know if I should. Kind of felt funny. I haven't been here in a while."

"Jack, you're almost kin. You might not have been home for twenty years, but you'll always be part of things here. Come on in." We moved through the kitchen. Like Mom's house – or maybe my house now, the thought scared me – what passed as the usual entrance and exit landed a person into the kitchen. It's always the center of the home, the place of community, where you gather for important times. Ray's kitchen still held that title, but I could see immediately that it was now a less energetic place, probably a place for a single man who didn't have any family here and clearly didn't seem to care about cooking. It was utilitarian, the place to make a sandwich but certainly not a place to stay. There was no mess on the counter, no bowl of fruit or vegetables to pluck from, no cast iron on the stove, only a single plate and coffee cup drying in the rack by the sink.

"Can I get you some coffee?" Ray inquired.

"No thanks. Had a little bit this morning already and truth be told I like those energy drinks when I need to do the morning shift. Seems to crank me up a bit more."

We meandered into the living room off the kitchen. This was definitely more inhabited. A little messier, like someone was living here. Magazines, mostly about rocks and gardening and hunting, were strewn about. There were copies of the weekly Kiowa paper, three or four versions of it, in various places about the room. The sofa and a sitting chair were on the other side from me and the center of attention in the room was the overstuffed recliner and a big fucking TV, maybe a 55-inch version. Man cave.

"You catch any of the game last night?" Ray settled into his chair as he asked.

"I take it you're still a Cardinals fan? I didn't see the game. Who won?"

Ray had been a passionate Cardinals fan for most of his life. While the TV surely brought him games now, I knew Ray had grown up on the nighttime signals of KMOX, the powerful radio station and affiliate network out of St. Louis. I tried it a few times, wanting to be like Ray, but it didn't stick. Baseball on the radio was even more boring than on TV. Radio generally sucked out here. FM was non-existent and the music on the dial was for the fucking elderly.

Ray had his heroes on the Cardinals. Bob Gibson was his hero. Then Lou Brock, then the great teams of the 80's. Cable got to him in the 90's and he could see his heroes in action on a regular basis rather than just the occasional vacation to Busch Stadium. All of those memories of Ray praising the Cardinals, the emotional ups and downs of every season, came back.

"They won in extras over the Mets. Carpenter hit a 3-2 pitch into the gap to score the winning run."

I had no idea who Carpenter was but smiled in agreement. "I don't really follow much baseball now, really any sports at all. The job keeps me hopping so most of my time is in the kitchen or thinking about the menu or other cooks. Actually, I haven't really had a vacation in a while. This is my first time away in years."

"Sounds awful. Well don't root for the Mets because they suck and the Yankees are an evil empire. You're good with the Cardinals or the Royals because it's where you're from, even if you don't know jack shit about the players."

We both laughed.

"Where's Beth? I thought she might be around."

"She popped down to the college. Did she tell you she might be looking at a job there? She has the formal interview tomorrow but she wanted to go down today and get a sense of the place. She hadn't been on that campus in a long time."

That was news to me. I couldn't hide my surprise.

"I didn't know. Well, she kind of made a wish that seemed like she wanted something new but I didn't know about this. That's cool, really."

"Tell her when she gets back. She left early and said she'd be back around now." There was a pause. I could sense a time to get to the heart of my visit.

"Ray, I really wanted to talk to you about Jill. I'm kind of in a bind and trying to figure out what to do. I know it's a lot but is there any way you could be involved?"

"What are you thinking?"

I paused. Normally with most people I'm a hard charger, kind of a brusque asshole really and say exactly what I want. In my head I could hear my words. "You take her because I can't deal with this shit." But I held back. In the pause, I slowed down and said something different. And without anger.

"I don't know. I mean, I'm pissed. This wasn't the plan because Mom was supposed to be around for a while. She got to deal with Jill and I got to live my life. It was settled or at least mostly settled and didn't need to think about it."

I kept on, searching for the next words.

"So my inclination is to want to find someone to take Mom's place so I can keep doing my thing. To find someone here, so I can go back to my life. I know that's asking a lot, but if I'm honest, that's what I really want. I don't want to be here. Too many bad things. Jill pisses me off. The farm feels limiting. All of it."

"Why?"

"What, why?"

"Why does Jill piss you off? Why is this limiting?" I had never encountered Ray like this. Maybe it was because we were both older and could tackle hard things as equals. He had always been easygoing Ray, fun Ray, Uncle Ray. This was a different Ray, maybe a lawyer. But it really wasn't. I sensed him interrogating me, but instead trying to help me come to grips with this situation, this moment, some new feelings.

"Jill pisses me off because she's so … she's so … infantile. I am dealing with a child there."

"Well, aren't you? Jill is in the body of a forty-year-old, but her development has been limited by not having interactions with many people over the years. That's who she is. You want her to be something else."

"But …" I trailed off because Ray's wisdom was lucid and competing with my own clouded garbage. To go further would be selfish.

"Ok. Granted. But I can't take care of a child. Not my gig."

"Can't or won't? Let me go back to your other comment. Why is this place limiting?"

"Easy. No good food. No culture. No interesting people, present company excluded."

"How do you know that? Truly, when's the last time you dealt with this full community? There are fascinating people around, in my opinion. Entrepreneurs, authors, managers, all of it. You've labeled something because of your impressions. And frankly, it seems snooty."

That motherfucker. I started to lash out and argue – because that's what New York chefs do – but something held me back. I think Ray saw an opening.

"Just like I have a bias that all New Yorkers are loud and kind of assholes, you have a bias that the people here are hillbillies. That we eat wrong. That we read wrong. That we don't listen to the right music. But I like these things more than what I might find in New York. I've found what's important to me here. If what's important to you is back east, then so be it. But really, truly, figure out what's important, not what makes you angry or feeds your bias."

"So I just come back here and be one of you?"
"Hear yourself. What you just said is rude. You say 'here' and 'one of you' like it's a bad thing. What is 'here'? What exactly is

'one of us'? ' Here' is my home where I've raised my child, had a wife, and I find peace in being able to garden and farm and play with rocks. And I'm one of them. I can do those things here and I don't think I can do those things there. So what do you value there so much that couldn't be here?"

"My job. My friends." And I stopped. My job is terrible and I only have one true friend in Derek. There really aren't others. So what did I value?

"Maybe you get it now?" Ray's voice had a soothing quality.

Silence. Then ...

"Jack, I'm dying."

I looked up and could see Ray was looking right at me. I wanted him to say more, to explain, to make the unreal more clear. But Ray let the silence sit. I spoke first.

"What's happening?"

"Congestive heart failure. The doctor saw it coming a couple of years ago, but it's accelerated in the last few months."

"Couldn't you get a heart transplant or something?"

Ray chuckled. "I love your 'or something' like a heart can magically be fixed."

"Well, can't it?"

"Not really. My heart is old and tired. It's just a little older and tireder than the other parts of my body. No shame in that. And to your other question about a heart transplant? The reality is I would be way down on the list because there are others who need it more. And I can't afford it. Well, I could sell all this land and still be left with a big medical bill. I don't want to leave that to Beth. I'd rather leave this farm. We've talked about it. She's sad but she supports it."

Ray spoke declaratively, like there wasn't any argument. It was a fact, clean and simple.

"How long?"

"A year give or take. I can feel myself slowing down. Spending a lot more time getting from one place to the next."

"What does it mean for your farm?"

"It's one of the reasons Beth is back. We're waiting to see if she gets the job at the college. If she does, she'll move in here. We'll have to find someone to cut the wheat, plant, all of that stuff but she'll take care of the home here, probably live here. If she doesn't get the job, she's talked about taking a leave of absence for the year. We'll see."

"So Jill …" I let it trail off.

"Yep, Jill. If my health were better, we could work something out. Even if it's a year, you'd be back in the same place."

I heard the car coming up the drive.

"Looks like she's here. Want to stick around for lunch?"

"I better get back." I could have stayed longer, I needed to get out, emotional distance and all. What Ray said was scary, not just his own situation but that he wasn't a solution for Jill. It wasn't anger or sadness that drove me to leave, just discomfort. It was a human reaction to someone's death story, right? What do you say to someone who's dying?

I heard Beth come through the door and soon she appeared in the living room. She seemed genuinely happy to see me, a big smile appearing on her face.

"Hey there! How are you today? Great time last night!"

I didn't return the smile. She was confused.

"It was." I turned to Ray. "I've got to get going. Thanks for the talk." Ray turned to Beth then.

"I told Jack I was dying."

Beth held Ray's eyes for a moment and swung them to me.

"Kind of a bummer, huh? I had the same reaction when he

first told me. But he's good with it. And in the end, if he's good, I'm good."

She wasn't being cavalier, only honest. There was a strength and willingness to accept Ray and the situation as it was.

"See why I told you I wanted to stay?" She said it to me with gentleness and grace, as an offering not of explanation but of emotional generosity.

Whatever it was about her, I softened. I looked at them both, first Beth, then Ray, back to Beth. My tension eased.

"You guys both are pretty good with it, aren't you?" They nodded in approval. Beth spoke up.

"It doesn't have to be a fight. It just, well, it just is. I'm going to be here for a while, one way or the other. I want to enjoy Ray and this wonderful place. If I can do it permanently, all the better. But it will happen how it needs to. No fight. Just moving forward."

A declaration. Then another silence. I was the first to speak. "I'm going to head home now. A couple of things." I reached into my pocket and brought out a closed fist.

"I have something for you, but I'll only give it to you if you come have a drink in town with me tonight. Deal?"

I offered her my opened hand. It was her wishing penny, flattened out, smooth and elongated.

"It was in the right place. Looks like your wish might come true."

18

BETH

Jack and I decided a drink was best. We weren't yet at the stage where dinner was "appropriate" for a date. Were we going on a date? There weren't a lot of options but Ray had recommended a new place in town, one of the very few that served something beyond Bud Light or some wine out of box that was generously called the "house" wine. The place was "Owen's" and Owen was a transplant from California.

We walked into a place that had no business being in a farm town on the Oklahoma/Kansas border. Modern décor, sleek lines, contemporary furniture, dropped lighting. The huge number of people on a Tuesday night was surprising and impressive. We found two seats at the bar which straddled the space between a very attractive and young-ish hostess and an open kitchen where a couple of cooks worked with intent.

And then Owen appeared. Well, I assumed it was Owen.

A middle-aged man, slim and bald with a goatee, completely out of place in Kiowa.

"A couple of newbies. I'm Owen, the namesake. What can I get you?"

"How did we stick out?" Jack seemed a little edgy, nervous almost. Me? Or the kitchen competition?

"Beyond your clothes, which look more like they belong on the coast, I know everyone who comes in, especially on Tuesday. You ain't them and you ain't dressed like them. Hence, a newbie."

His tone was smooth. The gleam in his eye said he had done this before.

"Guilty!" I said it with too much enthusiasm, like I was trying to cover for Jack. "Where y'all from?"

We looked at each other and laughed.

"Tough question," began Jack.

"Yeah, tough," I added. "We, uh … we both grew up here, farm kids, but left a while ago. I live in Ohio, he lives in New York City."

"Hey cool! I never did Ohio for any reason but spent a year in NYC working at a place on the Upper West Side. Fine dining, but shit, everything's fine dining there. What brings you back?"

I noticed Jack shifting about for a moment, looking down, trying to avoid the question. He went with the truth.

"Family. My mom just died. Lived out on a farm with my sister a few miles south of here. Got to take care of my sister. Got to plan the funeral."

"Hey man, bummer. My wife's dad died a few months ago. It was good we were around but it's hard to lose a parent." I kept thinking how practiced Owen was at this, that he wasn't speaking in platitudes, that he meant what he said. The mark of a good barkeep. I found that oddly comforting.

"And my dad lives just down the road from them," I said, pointing at Jack. "Came back to visit him. Ray Boucher? Know him?"

"Hell, yes! Great guy. Comes in maybe once a month. Sits

at the bar usually and we bullshit. Sometimes I call him 'the mayor'. One time he even brought me some mint to make juleps, around Derby time. He knows everyone. Been here awhile hasn't he?"

"Indeed, he has. This is home for him. And you … what brings you here Owen?" I could also do the bar conversation quite well, thank you.

"Well, that's a story that needs a drink. What are you having? We're not friends enough yet, so it's not on me, but maybe when we know each other better I'll slip you a free one now and then." His grin was inviting.

Owen took the orders - a Negroni for Jack, a perfect Manhattan for me - and set to work. A couple of minutes later, the drinks were sitting in front of us and Owen began his autobiography.

Owen had grown up in San Francisco, the only son of two architects, creative types who raised a son on art and ideas as well as counter-culture politics. He was interested in art, mostly sculpture and glassblowing ultimately took him to galleries and schools across the country. One of those stops was in Tulsa, where he met his wife at a bar. It was nothing other than seeing a beautiful girl, asking her to dance, and within a year they were married.

They got out of Oklahoma as soon as they could and headed back to California, this time in the LA area. Seemed like the right place at the time and his wife had a great opportunity to work in finance and investment. She started a lucrative career, he found a new love for cocktails and restaurants, and they lived a yuppie life. They loved the energy of Southern California but both could feel that something wasn't right.

After a time, both wanted out.

As heartless as it sounded, Owen described, Jenny's dad's

sickness gave them the reason to come back this direction. What started as a three-month hiatus turned into a year as he fought the disease. Eventually, Jenny lost her job. On the day it happened, both felt relieved, unencumbered. It was the last thing keeping them tethered to Los Angeles.

So they made it permanent. Jenny's dad passed away, they moved into the old house for good with Jenny's mom, and settled in. She got a job in a bank and loved it. He took some of their savings to start this place, thinking that everyone needed a place to get a good drink and interesting food.

"And you know what? We've got a kid due in a couple of months, we're building our own house next to Jenny's mom's place, and shit ... we're happy." Owen looked at Jack, waiting for a comment.

But Jack was quiet. I couldn't tell if he was intimidated by Owen's openness or if it was something else. Maybe it was just discomfort because people don't divulge like that in New York City. I filled the silence.

"What do you like about this place?"

"What's not to like? Ok, really, I get it. Small farm town near nowhere, Hicksville, no culture, a bunch of farm rubes. But here's the other side of the coin. Honest people. Authentic. I get to give joy through this restaurant and people genuinely appreciate it. There's no bullshit here. It's what I value. It's what I love. It's home."

Jack couldn't stay silent any longer. He pounced.

"So let me get at this ..." He said it with New York aggression, challenging Owen's rosy picture with his skeptical tone. But Owen's steadfast look held his gaze and seemed to soften Jack. He began again.

"I'm a little envious but also dubious. I cook for a living in the

City. Nothing fancy, but solid stuff, you know?"

"Cool. I knew I liked you for some reason." Owen had a way.

"But these people, like how could they appreciate good cooking or good cocktails?"

"See it differently. You're judging people. Get simpler. Why wouldn't people anywhere enjoy something great if you give them the opportunity? Just because they haven't seen it doesn't mean they won't be open to it."

Owen continued. "Let me try something on you. Why don't you like this place?" "The region? Because the people ARE idiots."

"And the folks in New York City aren't?"

Jack legitimately laughed and I laughed with him. "Point taken. But I know what I'm getting there. Here ... well, it just seems like there's something lacking. Like I couldn't have a conversation with anyone. What would I talk about, if it wasn't the weather or farming? God knows I couldn't talk about their pitiful politics."

"But have you tried? My guess is you're seeing it from a couple of different angles rather than opening up to more. You probably left as a pissed-off teenager and anywhere sucks when you're that age. Second, you live on a coast, and basically there is flyover state bias writ large. Anywhere but the coasts isn't worth shit. It's in movies, writing, everyday life. And it's just garbage. Give these folks a whirl. You might like the ride."

Owen turned towards a new couple that had just come in, late 50's or early 60's, overalls and boots and bad hats for both of them. He greeted them warmly and turned back to us.

"See them? He's a physicist, she's an engineer, both from Alabama. Wouldn't know that unless you asked. Just sayin' ..."

And with that he was gone.

We looked down at our empty drinks. "Should we get another one?" Jack asked.

"Probably so. Seems like we need another lesson from Professor Owen."

19

JACK

We ordered a second drink, which Owen delivered but he didn't stick around for more conversation. That didn't bother me a bit. The guy had cleaned my fucking clock and I was humbled but also pissed. I looked over at Beth.

"Look at this place. Who would have thought ..." I wasn't necessarily directing my comments to Beth but to the universe in general. "It's even in the details. Small tables, intimate lighting, even listen to the music for a second. Notice that?"

I could tell she hadn't paid any attention to these things but was intrigued.

"What about the music?"

"It's jazz but not too old or fussy. Sets the place as contemporary and hip, not old fashioned. And see the open kitchen? That's so people can connect to the food. It's not hidden and people can see it transforming themselves. Even look at the wait staff, how they're dressed. Black shirts, dark pants. Not a uniform per se, but enough that it differentiates the staff from the clients, and it gives off that same smell of cool as the music. It's all unified."

"And why are you amazed?" I could feel Beth's inquisition starting.

"Because this is not the kind of fucking place that should be in Kansas. It's a place straight out of the Village or Orange County or Seattle up on the Hill. Not here, but there."

"But doesn't Owen make a point? Aren't you assuming that people here wouldn't or couldn't like or understand this place? Seems you might be getting that wrong."

"Don't you think it's weird?" I was almost shouting. I paused and caught myself. "Sorry! I'm just having this visceral reaction to this place. And when I get past the weird, I love it. Holy buckets, I love it. Not just the food, but the assertion of what could be and the fuck-it-all attitude that makes it happen. And yeah, that people can love this at any time and any place if you do it right."

"What's your favorite movie?" It came out of nowhere.

"What? What's that have to do with it?"

"What's your favorite movie? Humor me. I have a suspicion."

"Probably Bull Durham. It's a baseball movie but it's not a baseball movie. It's about an old catcher working to make it to the big leagues but he gets called back to deal with some numbnuts pitcher. He teaches him. He teaches him the craft of baseball, not just a pitch or two, but how to really play the game, the nuances, the traditions. It's a respect for craft that I love."

"What else? How does it end?"

"The catcher quits the game and goes home to be with the lady who feeds his soul. He says he just wants to be, you know, he wants to just live in the moment and not feel pressured by the craft anymore."

She let the silence sit. She's good at that. When she started in, she looked right at me. "I don't know you well. But the bits

I've experienced with you seem to say that you love the craft of cooking. You love it. But I'd also venture that you don't really like where you are. You may not like who you are. It's not craft anymore. And you're looking and searching for a place where you can just be. Is that too shitty?"

"Keep going lady. I kind of like this."

"You love this place because you see a guy in Owen who can do his craft and just be. It's here. He couldn't do that in California but seemed to find a place here, a home, where it came together. Craft and being. Doesn't that appeal to you?"

"Yeah, sure. But not in Oklahoma or Kansas."

"Why not? I'm not even pushing for around here. I'm really just asking what this place has that is prohibitive."

What was it with her and the interrogation? The next question came out of nowhere.

"Why do you swear so much? The fucks and shits and bullshit. Why? You're a smart guy. So why? "

That pissed me off. It felt condescending. It felt critical. And I didn't want to be criticized. Especially by her.

"Because it's the way I fucking am." I said it with anger. She didn't back down one bit and fired back almost instantly.

"No you're not."

She said it in a way that disarmed me. Not with vitriol, like in the middle of a fight, not softly like she was trying to tame my anger. It was a declarative statement. Like "you breathe air" or "your hair is brown." You're not.

"Yes, I fu…" I stopped.

"No, you're not. I think you use it as a shield, a defense. It keeps people from getting close. I know, I get it, a NYC thing." She could see me mouthing New York City. "I've been there and people swear and talk with their hands and turn up the volume.

But you're not from there. You might live there but it's not your home. So don't swear. I'd like to get closer to you."

She smiled at me, inviting but with just a hint of sarcasm. "So what's prohibitive? I think that was the word you used about this place."

"I think you got me. I could say the people but there's you and Ray and Owen and the physicist and the engineer. I could say the culture but look where the hell –sorry–I am right now. I could say my mother but she's not here. So maybe it's just Jill."

"What's wrong with Jill?"

"She can't go anywhere."

"Is that her problem? Or is that your problem? Seems like that's her state of being. The only reason you don't like it is because now you have to change your life to fit hers. What if you just accepted that this is who she is. No more, no less."

I looked away. In truth, it was to hide my shame because she had hit the mark. So I deflected.

"What's your favorite movie?"

"Easy. To Kill a Mockingbird. Gregory Peck. It reminds me of good people getting at the tension of the world. Race and class, small towns and provincialism versus big cities and elitism, care for some and ignorance for others. I don't think it's a happy movie, only that there is and should be a spirit to be and fight for each other. I used to want to be Scout, then I modeled being Atticus, but at the end of the day it's Boo. I want to be Boo Radley. We should all be Boo."

"Is that too idealistic? I mean, I like it, but man New York City couldn't give two shi ... sorry, could give a fig about being decent to each other. We don't fight FOR each other, we fight WITH each other."

"So why are you there? That's not you. Or at least I think

that's not you. Is it you?"

She kept looking at me, deeply. No one had pressed me like this before, especially someone I didn't know the previous day. But I didn't want to be angry with her.

"You're good at this, aren't you? I'd love to show you some of my City whoop-ass right now but somehow I think I'd come out on the losing end. Is that the philosopher in you, this superpower to argue well and crush your enemies?"

She laughed. "Don't change the subject. Why are you still in New York? And you're better than that, right? And yes, I am a kick-ass philosopher who can win arguments. Don't try!"

It wasn't a fight in any sense, but there was a challenge in her words. I held her gaze this time and spoke softly.

"No, it's not me. You're right. My anger, my swearing, it's a defense mechanism, a way to cope in the land of the crazy and I feel like it's been eating me away for a while. But I really don't know where to go. That's not home, this isn't home, I don't have a home."

"You always have a home. Home isn't a place. It's where you decide to make it. It's where you build up your community, your posse. It's where you give sustenance to others and they give it to you. Geography doesn't matter."

"Where is it for you?" I asked this with a sense of urgency.

"Truly, I think it's here. I used to think it was any academic department or any university at all, but it's not. I can't find community where I am currently, so I need to look elsewhere. Ray's here. He's home. I do have a connection to the land, even though I don't think home has to be physically located. But it's that feeling with the land that keeps me here, not the land itself. Does that make any sense?"

I paused, thinking. "Yeah, it does make sense. I think about it from the perspective of an apartment or a house. It's not the physical thing, the house, but the sense of belonging there. I don't have that now, though I miss Derek. I had it once in a place in Portland. Townhouse, great neighbors, shared garden."

"Why did you leave? Who's Derek?"

"Derek. That's a longer story. Derek is my wonderful, not-gay, drag queen roommate. I love him. He's my best friend. And I left Portland because I had the opportunity to go to New York."

"And why New York if your home was in Portland?"

"Because that's what you're supposed to do as a chef. You go to New York. You cook great food and live the chef life." I stopped. "And truly it kind of sucks."

She let it sit again.

"Sometimes we don't have to chase the bright shiny thing when the thing that gives us vitality is simpler. We should chase what gives us hope and love and all those life-affirming possibilities. I'm done chasing academe. I'm going after something more."

"How do you do that?"

"I don't know. You just do. When we can confront the thing that we've been chasing and yell at it that it's no good anymore, seems like that can finally turn our attention. I don't know where I'm headed. I just know where I'm not headed any longer."

Later, after dropping Beth off I took a walk out to the barn. It was dark. The owls would be off hunting, together. But I wanted to be there and feel their presence. I crept up the stairs and softly sat down on a bale of hay. The starlight came through the openings on both ends. Shadows were everywhere, dark patches created and formed from present day objects and light from a million miles away.

The quiet was disarming. And yet comfortable. You couldn't

get this ever in the City. I let the peace settle over me. It was the "whoooo" sometime in the early morning that woke me up.

20

JILL

I got up real early today. I didn't feel strange about not having Mom around. I mean, get over it, right? And I had things to do! But Mom is usually, like, super noisy and I don't like all the quiet. It makes it feel dead and a little scary around here. So I went to see what Jack was doing down the hall. He'd make noise for sure.

I went down to his room and walked right in. I had to listen to see if he was alive. Yep, loud and clear and not even a hint of a snore or stuffed nose. So I kissed his cheek.

He woke up right away, like he was totally shot up out of bed. I think I saw that on Three's Company once when Mr. Roper got kissed by Jack on accident and shot up out of bed. It was so funny.

"Good morning sunshine! I was just checking to see if you were alive. Kind of a bad habit now after Mom died."

"What the f …? Are you going to do this every day?" Jack said this, like, with total exasperation.

"Probably. Although I'd rather you get up first and clank

around. That way I can stay in my bed for a while. It's what Mom did."

"Jill, I do not wake up early except when I have the morning shift. I do not like to wake up early. People should sleep until 10am at the earliest. Early morning is not beautiful. It's painful. Don't do this to me."

"Whatever. Want to make some pancakes together? I saw this great recipe last week and I think Mom got some buckwheat before she died."

I went off to the kitchen without waiting for an answer. I just knew he would follow.

"Did you have a nice time with Beth last night? Did you kiss her yet?"

"Stop asking. And I did not. We had a great time. She's pretty cool. Have you gotten to know her much?"

"Not really. I've seen her with Ray a couple of times before this but we didn't talk. I like her a lot though!"

"It's not just that. She's really insightful. Asks great questions. She's thinking about coming to live here with Ray. Did you know Ray's dying?"

"Of course I knew, Silly. Mom told me everything. I mean, who was I going to blab too, Martha Stewart? He told mom that a couple of months ago and then she told me. Mom was totally freaked out because she thought that Ray might take over when she was gone. I mean, Ray did that when Mom had to go out of town."

"Mom went out of town and left you?"

"Of course, Silly! She had doctor's appointments in Oklahoma City and would sometimes need to stay for two days when they did tests. Ray wouldn't actually stay here but he would check in every few hours and I had his phone number if anything came up. He would get me some food and things too. Ray's awesome. I'll miss him when he's gone."

Jack looked at me like I was crazy. Well, I would miss him. He's cool even if he smells funny.

"Aren't you sad that he'll die and you won't see him again?"

"Well sure. But everybody dies. I think it's especially good that we know when it might happen so then we get to say goodbye in a real proper way. Duh, Jack."

Jack laughed at me. Or at least I thought he was laughing at me.

"You're right Jill. It is better. You make things … simple." We started in on the pancake batter together. It was going to be so good. And we worked together real well in the kitchen, like I knew what he was gonna do and he knew what I was gonna. We didn't even need to talk. Oh my god, so cool. It was like we were in a restaurant kitchen. We got the cakes all up and they were perfect. I like mine with lots of syrup of course, especially because we didn't have any crème fraiche or strawberries. They are the only way to eat pancakes.

We started to eat and we talked mostly about food, about really awesome breakfasts, the shows I was watching, ingredients I had to have. It was great to be with my brother! But then he got real serious.

"You know Jill, the funeral is tomorrow, and then after that I'll need to leave to get back to work."

"No you don't."

I kept eating.

"Jill, I've got to head back. But we've got to figure out together how to deal with this. Is there any way you could move?" I got scared and put my eyes down on the pancake. I didn't want to talk anymore but he said something real quick.

"I'm sorry. I know you can't move and I'm sorry for even asking the question. It's just that I'm stumped. You can't move, I can't stay, Ray can't be here. My only thought is to get a home health person who could check in on you."

"I don't like that." I said it real flat and stared at my pancakes again.

"Why?"

"Because it's not you or Mom or Ray or someone I know. That's important to me , like real important."

"Come on, Jill. You could get to know that person. They would be great."

"And they might be terrible."

"Can we at least think about it some more?"

I got quiet. Jack was the one who was supposed to stay. We could make pancakes every day then and we could even see Beth. It would be awesome. But I was sad because it seemed like he didn't want to be with me. And that scared me lots.

And then I remembered.

I got up and went to my room. I reached way back into my closet, past all the issues of *Bon Appetit*, like twenty years' worth, and grabbed a big manila envelope. It had Jack's name on the front. I went back to Jack.

"Here. Mom said I was supposed to give this to you if she wasn't around. She said it was for if she didn't return from one of her trips. I didn't really think about it until now because she wasn't on a trip when she died." I went back to my room. Pancakes didn't sound so good anymore.

21

JACK

I opened the envelope. A few sheets of paper held together by a paperclip.

Ordinary paper, blank, like something taken from a copier. On the pages was Mom's gorgeous scrawl, intent and dark. It was one of her "letters". She had sent me a few of these over the years and sometimes I scanned them, most times not reading them at all and throwing them away. But I could have picked her penmanship out of a lineup. This letter was dated almost two years earlier.

Dear Jack,

It's a cliché … but you're reading this because I am gone. My guess is that I died in some horrible way, a car crash or an accident or something. Maybe that's my wish, to be taken from the world immediately. I don't want to linger, I don't want to hang around and wither. That would be a problem for a lot of people, especially me. I imagined suicide at one point, but I couldn't do it. It would have been the ultimate escape and I made my peace a while back to not do that to Jill.

As I write this, I've just been to the doctor. He gives me maybe five more years if everything goes right. As he says it, my heart is tired. There's not a disease and it's not a congestive thing, only that my heart as a muscle is tired and needs rest. When I asked why, he said it could be a lot of things but generally this usually involves too much exertion and stress. Basically your heart tires out if you work too hard or if you worry too much. I haven't worked that hard so I'm guessing it's stress.

I'm not ready to tell you in person about my heart issues. It's not time and you're still angry. I can guess what you're angry about and I'll get to that in a moment, but I can't talk to you through all your anger. If I told you I had heart problems and was going to die, I think you'd be angry at me. Not compassionate. Not feeling. Just angry. It's what I've gotten from you for the last twenty years.

At some level I get it. I've been angry for virtually your entire life. I've been a single mother with two kids and little emotional support. Ray and Ruth have been great over the years, just Ray lately, but it's not the same as having a partner to divide the work and divide the worry. That's been on me. I know, poor me, but it's worn on me, especially when there hasn't been relief for years.

Most kids grow up and move out of the house, but Jill never did. She stopped aging somewhere between the ages of ten and fifteen. I could never really figure it out. I went to some specialists to ask and they always said, "Bring her here so I can examine her." Obviously I couldn't do that and frankly no one was interested enough to come out and see her. They knew what it was, agoraphobia, and they told me there were lots of cases where the agoraphobia stopped any progress in a person's emotional development.

It's because there's no one else around to help them grow. No school, no friends, no teachers, no play outside, nothing. Without that stimulation they just stop and can only see the world through their current lens. The lens never changes for some. Even with books or with TV, nothing. It doesn't help. So Jill stayed that way even while she grew up physically. Sure, she picked up a few words and phrases, a little more knowledge here and there, but fundamentally I still had an adolescent daughter.

Imagine what it would be like to be with an agoraphobic teenager for a lifetime. I know, selfish. But imagine what that's like. You can love them and be with them, but you feel trapped. I felt trapped. Her agoraphobia became attached to me as well. She loved this place, this home, because it was her shelter and protection from the outside world. I hated this place because it was my prison. I could never escape. Not for a vacation, not for a respite, nothing. It was always here when I came back.

That took its toll. At least that's what I think happened. It's the story I tell as the reason for my health. I took all that anger and all that stress and made it stick until it kills me. And it will kill me. There's no reversal and the doctor says that my five-year window might last longer or it might be shorter but his best estimation is five years. It will really start to show in two years and then there will be a time when I won't be able to get out of bed until I just stop. So I promise to tell you about it in two years. Unless something happens before that so I'll tell you now.

Here's the other thing. I am less angry now that I see what's in front of me. It's no way to live a life. That's part of why I'm writing you. You'll undoubtedly be angry that I've passed away and now you have to deal with Jill. I understand it's an intrusion on the life and home you've made. But you were angry before that. Angry at me and angry at Jill. You seemed especially angry at Oklahoma. Every time I asked you to come back and visit, inevitably you would say something about not wanting to visit "that shithole."

I stayed angry for too long and it hurt me in ways only now I can come to grips with. It limited me from friends and it limited me from possibilities. It wasn't Jill that was limiting. It was me. I could have had a better life, even with Jill. I just chose not to. It helped justify my anger. But no more of that for me.

I hope not for you either. Whatever anger you're holding onto is not real. It just allows you to be a certain way to the world. But it's not who you are. I know that. I think you know it, too.

So Jill. Beautiful, wonderful Jill. There's the real point of the letter. What are you to do about Jill? Start with this. Whatever rational thought you have that she will be able to go somewhere else, get it out of your head. She cannot. Even if you would drug her and move her elsewhere, you would be ripping her from this house. And truly, very truly, I think she will go crazy. She will likely kill herself at the first opportunity because she simply can't live elsewhere. That's the reality. Accept it. Don't fight it.

Also accept that she is amazing. We have to take her as she is, not as we want her to be. We want her as a functioning and rational adult. She is not. Accept that. She is a teenager with unbelievable cooking skills. And memory. And joy. You've never seen any other teenager like her. If you accept that, she suddenly becomes so much more in your eyes. Not a burden, not a responsibility, but a joy.

So what do you do? I can't answer that for you. Someone could come and stay with Jill. Somehow that doesn't seem right. She's family, not some pet you get someone to leave water for and clean up after you've headed on vacation. She's not a kennel animal. She's a kid. She needs someone she knows and trusts. She loves Ray, but Ray I think is probably a stop gap. I can see him winding down just like me. No, Jill needs you. She trusts you. It's the unshakeable teenager thing. She grew up with you and loves you. You could have moved half the world away, shaved your head, become a monk, but she still sees you as her unchanging brother, the one who has been with her and for her all her life. Why do you think she cooks? It wasn't until she knew you were a chef in Portland that she started to cook and watch all her shows. And when you moved to New York, she was sure you were going to get your own TV show. Actually, she still thinks that!

I think I do have a right to ask so I will. Will you come home now?

Love, Mom

There was one more sheet in the pile. I noticed the date was one month ago.

Dear Jack,

My time is almost up. I saw the doctor yesterday and he told me I have less than six months to live. My condition has accelerated. I haven't had the courage to tell you yet even though I said I would. I tried to call a moment ago but only got your voicemail. I didn't leave a message. This topic doesn't seem fit for a voicemail.

I am not angry at all now. Just in peace. I know Ray is dying also and we've found some comfort in each other, telling each other our deepest secrets and our deepest worries. I told him I once had a crush on him. He laughed and said he had one on me also but he met his wife at a party the next week and never asked me out. We both wondered what might have been.

I want you to come home. It's important not just to Jill anymore, but to me. We need to hold hands and hug one more time. Just one more time.

I'll keep trying to call. Maybe even get my courage up to leave a message or write a letter.

I love you. We - Jill and I - need you here.

Mom

I closed the letters. Mom's words had defused my anger. Whatever was left was pretty raw. Maybe sadness, maybe hurt, probably guilt because of some missed opportunity, Look, my mother hadn't ever done anything violent or terrible towards me. No, it was the accumulation of years of her having to pay all her attention to Jill and giving me none. She would snap at me, order me around, but maybe I quit trying to talk to her. Maybe I quit trying altogether. Damn, I just wanted to talk to her now

I remembered, now, a few hang-ups on my voicemail the last couple of weeks and a disembodied caller on the other end of the line who wouldn't say anything. Each time I saw it was an undisclosed number from Oklahoma, but I assumed it was some telemarketer in Tulsa or a salesperson who had taken my name from the voting rolls that weren't up-to-date. It was her. And that made me even more sad. That I hadn't spoken to her. That she couldn't say anything.

I put the letters back into the envelope and walked to Jill's room. I knocked softly and heard her say "come in". I began to speak, but decided that maybe words weren't needed for either of us. Instead, I took her hand. I didn't say anything for a long time. Neither did she.

At some point, she went to sleep, unlatching her hand from mine, but wanting me to stay and watch over her. She had never done that in the past. But I wanted to. I wanted to protect her, to be with her, that somehow it was important for us to be together. Maybe it was Mom's words, maybe it was Jill's silence, maybe it was just the right thing to do.

My reverie was broken by the buzzing phone in my pocket. It was Derek. Man, just when I needed him most. I slipped out the door, gently placing my hand on Jill's back as I went to the hallway and shut the door.

"Derek? Hey, it's me. Give me a sec. I've got to get to a quieter place. Jill is sleeping."

I went into the kitchen and sat at the dining room table.

"Hey, it's great to hear from you. I miss you. Do I get to say that to my best friend?"

"Well, good morning sunshine!" Derek's big voice exploded out of the phone. "That's new for me. You are usually one big ball of gruff. Did you pick up a sensitive gene somewhere en route to the middle of nowhere? I miss you too. Just wanted to check in and see how you were doing with everything."

I cackled. It was vintage Derek to call me a ball of gruff, but it was also that Derek could immediately sense the weight of the world on my shoulders. Derek was good about that, wanting to make me laugh and ease back a bit.

"I'm ok, better now that you've called. It's been tough. Let me give you the highlights."

I proceeded to describe the last couple of days, especially the frustration of not knowing what to do about Jill and the dilemma with Ray. I also mentioned my time with Beth, our walk and then drinks in town, and finished with a play-by-play of Mom's letter. "Basically, she's telling me not to be angry, she's sorry, that Jill's ok and perhaps I should really think about coming here to be with her. And every time I do think about it, it pisses me off."

"Jack, honey, you're violating your mom's first rule of fight club: don't be pissed. Second rule, don't be pissed at Jill. Third, there's a letter here for you. Big guess is it's from your mom."

"Save it. Not the comments, the letter I mean. Don't worry about opening it but just toss it on my bed. I've got a pretty good idea what's in there already. And your comments, how can I not be pissed? This is a real problem, growing bigger and I don't have a solution. What would you do?"

"Not be pissed, knock Jill's ass out, and move her back to the City!"

Again, vintage Derek. He said it without a trace of irony, completely stone-faced like he was saying a fact of life. I knew he was playing me.

"I can't afford drugs like that, Jill would go crazy or I'd kill her along the way, and then I'd end up in jail and I can't cook there. So that's out."

"So, I'd stay."

Derek also said this in his matter-of-fact way. He was serious. Silence sat between us over the phone. Derek interrupted first. "And about this girl Beth? Let's talk, brother."

"What about her?"

"Don't play like that! You go on a farm walk with her, you go out on a date and have drinks, my guess is maybe a kiss."

"It wasn't a date and there was no kiss. She's a philosophy professor for God's sake. I cook, she reads Plato or Aristotle or some shit."

"But you kind of like her, huh?"

Derek knew exactly how to get to the heart of it.

"I hear it in your voice. Dude, I know you. You're trying to gloss over or some shit but she's there and seems like an important part of the story. You're playing it cool. Don't. It doesn't become you."

I knew he was right. No need to deny it.

"Yeah, she's cool. She grilled me when we went out for drinks in a way no other woman has done before. Called me on the carpet. But rather than fight, which is my normal barbarian way of handling things, we just talked."

"Let the logic win, brother!"

Derek could do that with me, pulling out of me what was going on when I didn't know it myself.

"So when's the next date?"

"I don't know. She's going down for an interview at the local university. She might be moving back here. Her dad is dying and she wants to be around, but she really seems to like it here."

"Why?"

"She says it's around a connection to the place and to the people. That somehow it feels more personal, more authentic. Ok, I'm paraphrasing, but it's like she's in a part of the world - her academic world and the place in Ohio - where she doesn't know what's real there. Here she knows what is. Kind of cool, really."

"As opposed to New York which is either profoundly authentic or profoundly a fraud?"

"What do you mean?"

"Come on, dude. This place sucks. It's either that a person has no filter and is authentically raw or makes up shit and puts on a face - which of course I love, because I can wear women's clothes. I'm both and that's why it works for me. But I get it. Iowa has something like that I think. You know exactly what you're getting. It bored me to tears of course but two thumbs up for consistency if that's what you're into."

"Maybe I am into that and just don't know it. Being here, well I've had the urge to fight like I always do in the City, but something keeps bringing me down. It's Jill, it's Beth, it's Ray, it's my mom's letters ... something's calming me."

"What does that mean?"

"Nothing. Yet. Right now it means that I've got to figure out what to do about Jill. The funeral is tomorrow and I probably need to be back to work by the end of the week."

"Do you have to be back to work?"

"Yeah, probably, I mean, I should."

"Dude, get it right. 'Should' means it's not about you, that it's for your asshole manager. What do you want?"

Again, silence. Derek had pricked my defenses.

"I think I want to be back. I just want normal. I want to deal with my life, not Jill's, and not here."

"Uh, hello there, best friend! Duh. Jill is your life. She's not something separate. And what do you mean, I think I want to be back? That's weak."

"What are you saying?"

"Here's the deal. You've hated your current job for a while. You get angry and complain about New York. You don't love it. You just exist. Me, I love this place and never want to leave. You? You're just here because you don't know where else to go or what to do next. You came to the City to be a cook. Good for you, check that box. But that isn't living, it's just achieving. It's time for you to go. Go live again."

"Where? How?"

"Doesn't make a difference. I mean, it does eventually, but not right now. Call up your job. Tell them you need more time. Who cares if they say no? If they do, quit. You'll always get a job because you can cook your ass off. But see this time right now as a gift. Take it."

Derek. Derek who spoke truth.

"I got to get you and Beth together. My two philosophers."

"Where's Jill?"

"Sleeping. Want to call back later?"

"Yeah. Tell her I love her. Dude, I love you too. Know it. Now I'm hanging up so you don't have to say it back."

I heard the click. I put the phone down and started away, but two steps later I was back, phone in hand. I dialed.

"Manny speaking. What can I do for you?"

"It's Jack."

"Where the fuck are you? I thought you'd be back by now. Oh yeah, how's your sister? The funeral?"

"The funeral is tomorrow. My sister's been hard. I need a

few more days."

"How many, Jack? It's balls up here."

"Sometime next week, maybe Monday or Tuesday. I just don't know."

"Jack, I need you back before then. If the funeral's tomorrow, then get on a plane on Friday. Weekend rush coming. Festivals and shit here in town this weekend."

"Can't do it."

"Can't or won't?"

It was a challenge. I heard it in his voice. I got pissed, quick. "Can't because I won't. Fuck you Manny, my mom died. You think I need to fucking work to take that off my mind?"

"You saying you won't be in this weekend?"

"I am. After that, I don't have a plan yet. I'll let you know when I do."

"Jack, that won't work. Either you're here or you're not."

"Then I'm not. No ultimatums. I don't do that shit."

"You're done."

It wasn't a question from Manny, it was a statement. "Sounds like I am. Send my last check to my address." I hung up. And beneath my anger, I felt freedom. I needed to tell someone. So I called.

"Beth, hey, it's Jack. Just wanted to see how your interview went this morning." She seemed both stunned and pleased that I was calling.

"Well, hello! Yep, just back from the interview. It went well I think. I met with the department chair and a couple of faculty colleagues. They want me to come visit again on Friday to meet with the VPAA and President. That feels like an offer is coming."

"Good for you! What the hell is a VPAA?"

She laughed, either in appreciation for my honesty or for my stupidity. Probably both.

"It's a Vice President for Academic Affairs, basically the boss of all the faculty. That's the person that usually makes job offers. This one's a little different because I'm around and they want to meet in person. Normally these things happen over the phone but I'm here and I sense their desperation! The karma's good I think."

"Good for you! I kind of got fired this morning."

"What does that mean?"

"Quick replay: I talked to Derek, my roommate. He shoots straight and basically told me I need to take some more time here to sort out my situation with Jill. He's right. So I called my boss who essentially gave me an ultimatum when I asked for more time. I said stick it and here's where you send the last check."

"Good for you!"

I don't think her response could have been more validating. But I still hesitated, like I needed to verify her support. "Why good for me? I'm jobless, my mother just died, and my agoraphobic sister has no keeper other than me."

"It is good for you! I assume you can get a job any time you want with your cooking skills. So sometimes we need space to figure it out and jobs can be stifling. I came home to that. Maybe you did too."

"Yeah, well, maybe."

"Maybe, nothing. Hey, how about this? I'll see you at the funeral tomorrow and we can talk more about the next steps. But let's make a date for Friday. Why don't you come with me to the interview - well, not the interview itself - and we'll celebrate with lunch afterwards. You drive. I like your rental car better than what Ray's got for me."

"Done. I'd love that. You choose the place, the greasier the better."

We hung up. I turned around and noticed Jill in the kitchen doorframe.

"Jack's got a girlfriend, Jack's got a girlfriend!" She said it in a sing-song way, like a child would have, when teasing a sibling. I wasn't offended.

"No girlfriend, just a friend. But maybe. We'll see." And I walked past her and into the rest of the day, perhaps with more lightness than I had experienced in a while. Maybe Oklahoma and a girl will do that to you.

22

JACK

The funeral for Mom was a quick affair. It was a graveside service and the audience was small. The pastor from the church she had once attended gave a stock eulogy, the kind of thing that didn't have any spirit and had been in every movie and tv show. Typical stuff about being one of God's children, being in a better place, we cannot know why and should only accept God's grace and will.

Normally I would have been ultra pissed at this. It is exactly the kind of thing that sets me off. Inauthentic language, a eulogy meant to comfort but making no sense, all of it. It reminded me of a time with Derek when we saw some off-Broadway show, a friend of a friend of a friend of Derek's who had written his heart out with this magnificent opus that had to be seen. The play was terrible, but I was especially turned off at the funeral scene where the main character's lover had been egregiously crushed in a car accident. The pastor there said the same things.

"Why do they even say that? It's bullshit!" I had proclaimed to Derek after the play.

"What do you mean?"

"That eulogy crap. It doesn't mean anything. Why say it? Instead, maybe say that it totally sucks that someone passed away and we have no fucking idea where they are, only they're not here anymore and it's crap. That's what should be said."

Derek looked up at me. "It's because we're not certain what to say. We need to fill the space and we don't know what to say."

"Then don't say anything!"

"What would be better? Some words or no words?"

"At least silence would be better than filling the space. That way we could at least be with our own anger."

"Dude, look, I feel you. Anger and sadness at those moments are on overdrive. I get it. The words are hollow. But silence just lets it sit. Sometimes it's better to fill the void with something rather than nothing. It pushes out the crap. The most important thing is what comes after the crap. That's where truth lies."

That was what I remembered most when I was asked to speak after the pastor.

The church for Mom's service wasn't on a hill or at some obvious place. It came at the crossing of two dirt roads, a two- room building, one room for saying and praying, the other for eating and meeting. To the side was the graveyard, sectioned off by a lone arbor entrance, no fencing around it, only an opening to walk into the space that seemed to signify you were passing from a place of light at the church to a place of darkness. And clearly the congregation hadn't been that big ever because there were only a handful of markers, maybe thirty or forty at best. But that was huge in comparison to the audience for this service.

I stepped in front of everyone to speak and the only faces I knew were Beth and Ray. The rest -- maybe ten or twelve —

consisted of what I assumed were church members, acquaintances of Mom, about the same age, about the same presentation. I hadn't known what to expect. Mom went to this church sometimes but I never asked what the relationship might be, how often she went, who she knew, what ministries she participated in. I always assumed it was limited because of Jill. And then I started to speak.

The evening before, I'd tried to pen something. Public speaking isn't my thing so I had to prepare. The last thing I did was a presentation on AIDS in high school. I read directly from a script and that assured me an A because really Ms. Bernhower gave an A to every graduating senior in her class. Regardless, this was my reference point. I needed a script. But what came out of my writing was trite, similar to the unknown pastor before me. I kept at the writing but nothing emerged. So I quit. This morning I went at it again but finished with the same result. Nada. I thought I could push it until later when I was in the car on the way to the funeral but that yielded squat. So here I was, staring out at the audience without having a single word prepared to say about Mom. That silence was really uncomfortable, but really, I was just scared. I couldn't find words. So I fell back on the truth. And just started talking.

"I'm locked up really. I don't know what to say. I tried to write some things yesterday and today. I'm usually pretty good with words, even when I don't swear." The audience chuckled. It loosened me up.

"But here I can't swear – at least I think I shouldn't with the pastor right there – and I'm not talking about cooking. I'm talking about my mom … and my mom's death … and what she meant to me, and maybe what she meant to you."

I kept searching for words. I heard one parishioner rustle and then saw the pastor move towards me, to comfort me, like he thought my silence was related to tears. It wasn't. I started in again before he got to me,

"I think I've only known my mother through opposition. And when it's that way, we probably don't think well of that person. I haven't. I had fights with my mom and resented her since I was a young kid. I kept fighting her through high school and then left as soon as I could. I've hardly been back, I've hardly seen her, and I really didn't want to. I don't know that I have much to say because I didn't know her. If I did, it was only through my sister's eyes."

That didn't sit well with the audience. They wanted to revel in the goodness of the person passing away, some anchor of comfort similar to what the pastor had provided, and I wasn't giving them that. I looked at Beth and she mouthed, "It's OK. Keep going." I needed that.

"That's my direction. If I didn't know her, then my sister knew her well. It's probably better that you hear her words. Her impressions. Because that's where the real power lies in my mother."

The discomfort -- mine and the audience's -- started to melt away.

"Most of you would know or have some sense of my sister Jill. She's a little bit older than me but she's an agoraphobe. She stays in, she never goes out. Imagine that. Imagine never having the opportunity to go out, living in a cage. But she doesn't see it like that. No. Instead, she sees it as her home. The place she exists. It gives her comfort and strength and a reason to be. Now imagine the caretaker of that person."

"Imagine the immense burden that presents. The person you're caring for can't go out, can't fend for themselves for the most part, can't shop, can't get a job, can't go away on a vacation, can't go to the doctor, and can't make friends because there are limitations on the social interactions. Imagine it. You are that person's everything. You provide everything. And it's relentless. No end."

"That's the life my mom had. I don't know if she told you. Maybe she did. But my guess is she didn't. She shouldered the burden and didn't open up to many. She came to church and I'm sure that was an escape for her. Maybe a time or two in town, but beyond Ray over there I don't think she had many people. Her life was one of service. And it was lonely."

"So how do you talk about that life? That's been on my mind lately. I came here angry three days ago. But maybe I've come round. I came here scorning her life, wondering what the hell she was doing, and wondering what I was going to do now. But maybe instead of scorn, my attitude should be one of awe and honor. Honor her life. Honor her sacrifice. Honor her ability to serve someone else so deeply and fully. We just don't see that much anymore. I guess I don't see that much anymore."

I was close to tears listening to my own words. It freaked me out a little bit. I'm male and we as a segment of the species rarely cry, right? But I think I wasn't talking to the crowd any longer. I was talking to myself. I was creating a new perspective of Mom, of Jill, of life.

There are moments, sincere moments, when life changes. These moments are generally about when what we have seen and done before, is suddenly, yes, most suddenly, created in a new way. It opens us up, it shifts our thinking, and forms some path to a new possibility. And it was happening to me. I was able to see most of "this", whatever "this" actually was, in a new way. I could see my current life as fraudulent, that my years as a chef were never about serving people and bringing them joy but really was about my own self-satisfaction. I didn't really care about anyone other than Derek. "I work as a chef. I make food, sometimes great food, and I think I'm doing it because I can make others happy, that I can serve them. But I don't think that's authentic. We serve when we devote ourselves to others, when we turn our attentions and our actions to the good of somebody who isn't us. Are humans inherently selfish? Maybe. The cliché is that we've got to take care of ourselves before we take care of others. Perhaps that's wrong. Maybe we take care of ourselves by taking care of others."

I looked at the crowd and could tell that maybe I was going too far. Except for Beth. She was beaming. I also knew I couldn't be working out this newfound life philosophy in the form of a eulogy. I veered back to course.

"That was Mom I think. She worked this out. She was angry also at some point, but I know, I just know, that she got to a place where she took care of herself by devoting herself authentically andJill. That's a life well lived."

I paused and looked out over everyone. "May we all live lives in that way." I said one more thing which had never come to my lips before. Ever.

"Amen"

The crowd murmured "amen" in response. After the crowd had moved on, Beth approached me. "Really powerful stuff. My instinct says that's not what you usually do. And it was perfect. You honored your mom with your honesty."

I looked at her and could tell she wasn't just trying to make me feel good. She was speaking truth. She was proud of me.

"Thanks. It was honest, I think. Usually my honesty comes out as anger or sarcasm. It came out differently this time. I kindof like it."

"Me, too." As she said it, she reached out and took my hand. It wasn't awkward, just nice. And natural. At least that's what I thought. We held it there for a moment or two until it seemed time to drop it.

"Hey, you want to come back with me to the farm? I want to visit with Jill and tell her about the funeral."

"I'd love to. Let me go tell Ray to head back on his own and I'll come with you. Sound good?"

"You ever wonder how time passes out here?" I said rhetorically as we drove, like I was seeing the land and the wheat in a different way. But Beth took me at a literal level.

"Not really. I guess when you mention it, time does seem to be slower here. But it's not boredom for me. It's just an ease, a lassitude, something that slows me down as well. You?"

"You know this, but it makes me uncomfortable as sh... It makes me uncomfortable. But it's shifting, you know? I can't figure out if it's me that's just giving in, which of course, I fu–I hate, or if somehow time being slower is making me think differently, act differently, sort of be differently."

"I mean, we've been around each other only a few days and in weird circumstances, but even over that time, you seem ..." She trailed off, looking directly at me and searching for the right word. "Settled. You feel at peace. Like you don't know what to do with Jill, but rather than it being a chore or a task, it's a challenge."

I let two dirt crossing roads go by before speaking again. "Can someone change that way, that quickly?"

"I didn't know there was a rule or expectation about that. Is there some standard time frame for people to be impacted by a different world or a different perspective? I mean, people see horrible instances on TV or experience something drastic and from that day forward they're a different person."

"But is that me?"

"Could it be you? Sure. Seems like you're open to it at least."

We drove into the circle driveway and parked in front of the house, next to the kitchen.

"Jill, honey? I'm back. Beth is with me."

"I'm in here, watching some Food Network. Great one withGuy Fieri. He's got some serious diners and dives on this episode."

We went into the living room and saw the spiky haired restaurant critic on TV, tasting some concoction and raving about it.

"The funeral was really nice. Want to talk about it?"

"Not really. I mean, I've seen funerals on TV and they're all somber and people talk and say nice things about the dead person. Not my cup of tea, no, sireee."

"Even though it was Mom's funeral?"

"Especially because it was Mom's funeral. She was awesome, but she's gone. I'm ok with it now and I want to remember her in a great way. I don't want to be sad even though I'll miss her like crazy. I just want to be happy that I got to be with her so long and that she was a Super Mom!"

I smiled at that. "Jill, you are smart. That's exactly right. No need to feel so sad, just be fine with what's going on here and remember the good stuff, right?"

"Right!" Beth chimed in. "So what should we do to celebrate her with with you, Jill? Everybody else got the funeral, but what could you do?"

Jill thought for a second.

"I know! Let's make Mom's favorite meal together. All of us -- you and me and Jack. We could even invite Ray."

"What was her favorite? I'm a little embarrassed, I don't know." I hesitated, like I should have had that information.

"Don't be embarrassed, Silly. You wouldn't know at all because she never told you. She told me. It's chile rellenos."

"What? Where did that come from?"

"Two places. She told me once that the true love of her life was a boy that she could have run off with when she was eighteen or nineteen. She didn't because it didn't seem sensible. Anyhooo, their favorite meal together was chile rellenos at a Mexican place in Enid. Also, she loved it when I was on my Mexican food kick a few years ago. Remember that?"

"I do remember that. I think you called and told me it was because you had been watching some shows with Rick Bayless, right?"

"That's totally right! I made rellenos one night and she asked me to make them again the next night. And then we had them like once every two weeks until lately. It's her favorite." I looked at Beth who nodded in appreciation. She spoke up. "Ok, what's a relleno? Is that sort of like a taquito?" Jill was the one who chimed in before I could.

"A relleno is this totally awesome green chile that is stuffed with cheese, usually and other stuff and then deep fried and you put on sauce and it's, like, super good."

I spoke up then. "You know it sounds like bar food, but a relleno, when done well, can be fine dining. Stuffed with chanterelles and topped with pomegranate seeds and walnut sauce, I've seen them go for thirty dollars a plate in New York."

Beth held up a hand. "Ok that sounds awesome, but I want the bar food version. Deep, deep fried, ok? I'll get Ray and the margarita fixings. Jack, you get the ingredients we need if they're not already here. Meet back at 7pm and it'll be a party."

Much later, only the liquefied remnants of margarita were left in the blender. "Want it?" I pointed at the blender and motioned to Beth. Ray and Jill were off in the living room.

"Let's split it."

I poured it into two small cups and handed one to her. I needed one last toast for the evening and raised my glass. Ray had been relentless, even Jill had chimed in with a good one asking us all to toast to Mom's love of "more BAM!" like Emeril.

"Here's to slowing down and maybe finding a new way."

Our glasses clinked. It struck me that we each had an individual journey ahead. But I also wondered what that might look like together.

23

BETH

The trip to Alva was no different than the one to Kiowa, only ten minutes longer. It's all dirt roads and wheat fields until you hit pavement. No trees in sight. We made a quick pass through Capron where Ray had been to school, kindergarten through twelfth grade. I knew Jack didn't go there because the school closed when we were kids. Not enough families and children to sustain it.

"You ever spend any time here?" Jack asked me. He was looking at all the abandoned buildings that dotted both sides of the main road.

"Not really. Maybe a time or two stopping at the gas station. Not much here." I pointed out a decrepit building, one that seemed to be slouching towards the ground under the weight of its own age.

"Yeah, me too. No other reason to be here. Most of the kids here went to Alva for school, north of here to Kiowa. Didn't really know anyone."

"Ray had a good friend who lived here. He told me as a kid he came down here pretty regularly to play whiffle ball or work on cars. Told me they got in a lot of trouble. He ended up a doctor in New Mexico and then they lost touch."

"Even doctors can come from here? Yeah, different world then. Could you imagine being here with just not much to do at all?" I paused.

"Maybe. I know that sounds weird, but I think I could be real happy with my books, a garden, a couple of good friends. I don't need that much anymore. You?"

"That sounds awful." I could see him thinking.

"But you know..." He trailed off then began again. "You know, for all of it, I don't have or need that much. I cook - or cooked, now - in a restaurant, I have one really good friend, I spend my off time at grocery stores or looking through cookbooks. I mean, all that other NYC stimulus doesn't do much. It's just noise. So I guess I could do something like this if those things were available. It's an interesting thought experiment."

"Well, it might be reality for me. I think the interview today is really just a job offer. I can't imagine them dragging this out. They need someone, I'm qualified. It's going to happen. And unless I get some weird vibe from the people today, I'm going to say yes."

"You're really gonna do this?"

"Yep, really and truly. I told you I don't like Ohio and this always feels right." I pointed out the window and spread my hands. "I'm more at peace here. Ray needs me and I need him in his last years. For what it's worth, I think I can make a difference with the students here in a way I can't in Ohio. Those are private school kids. It's finishing school. These kids at Northwestern are farm kids, straight off the tractor or the ag business. They can read books and have ideas. You were one of those kids once."

"Kind of audacious, isn't it?" Jack said this with a sly grin. It felt more like support than criticism.

"Probably. But why not? What about you? What would be audacious for you?"

Jack took a moment, still thinking. "Audacious for me would be … opening up my own restaurant. I think every chef thinks about it but no one really jumps. It takes a lot of money and a lot of balls."

"Why?" I was curious.

"The money part is heavy. It's usually in the hundreds of thousands of dollars. There's equipment and decor, but also licenses and inspections and staff. It's spendy. The courage is doing that and knowing it will probably fail. Most do."

"So people don't do it because they might fail?"

"Yeah, basically."

"Well, that's stupid."

"Stupid, why? Seems kind of smart to me. Why waste all the money?"

I wanted to challenge him. "No, no. I get the money part. Any big investment like that is hard. No, what I meant by stupid is how wrong that orientation is. When we don't do things because they might fail, it's …" I was looking for the right words. "It's playing to lose or not playing at all, really. To live, we have to play. If we don't play, we don't live. Make sense?"

"Sure, but why risk the money?"

"That's not it. I'm asking, why risk anything at all? Because if we don't risk, we never reward. Ok, an instinct here. Did you have a job when you moved to Portland?"

"No, I was young and dumb.'

"Young, yes ... dumb, no. If you had chosen not to risk, then you wouldn't have gone at all. You had the chance to fail and not get a job. But you didn't. You risked and you went there. Got the first job obviously and it led to your current job in the City."

"My ex-current job in the city."

"Yes, granted, your ex-job. But we live when we risk. Not stupid risks, but real risks that have as much chance to succeed as fail. I'm risking taking this job. I likely can't get another job in academia after this. Not that I want to, but this is a dead end."

"So why are you doing it? Why take the risk?"

"Because I can be safe and get tenure at my current job. I can be there for a lifetime. But that's not playing to live. This job, this allows me to live. And if I'm great at it -- which I will be of course! — then I have joy. If I stink, so what? I played. If my joy goes or I stink, then I'll take a risk and go do something else."

I was challenging him more directly. He looked out the windshield to avoid me. I did the same.

"What would it mean to open up a restaurant here?"

"As in, *Oklahoma* here?"

"Sure. Owen did it with his place in Kiowa."

"I would need a space."

"What's that look like?"

"Depends on what I want to do. If it's volume, then I need a high traffic area, somewhere that people already go and will stop in. You know, town square or next to shopping or a movie theater."

"And if it's not that?"

"Could be mostly anywhere if it's a destination. Basically,

you go there just for the experience."

"Which do you want?" I was forcing the issue. Jack clenched his jaw, then let it go. "You're a pistol, aren't you?" He grinned as he said this. "Yes, I am, thank you." I replied.

"I want the latter. I cook–'scuse me–*used to* cook--at the former. It's not a 'destination' place. It's the place people who live on the Upper West Side come to eat when they aren't going to a destination place. The traffic is there. Don't get me wrong, the food is superb. But people know what they're getting. The bar is low for experience."

"So why the latter?"

"I'm getting there. Patience, good lady!"

I wondered if he had had this conversation with anyone but himself. I also wondered why it was with me.

"I want to cook my food, not someone else's. A lot of people think chefs cook what they want, that it's an expression of themselves, artistry. The number of chefs who do that is miniscule. They're on TV or profiled in magazines, but the vast majority of us cook what someone else has told us to cook. It's not us. It's from some faceless person in the sky. OK, yeah, I get to put my spin on eggs Benedict ,but really, it's eggs and sauce. If I was doing it myself there would be some edge to it, something different."

"So why not do that?"

"You asked for the dream, not what I'm doing."

"And I'm asking why not do that? It's that risk thing again. Now is the time. You don't have anything tethering you."

"Yes, I do."

"What? New York? Derek? New York is a place you cook, not your home, from what I can see. Derek is a great friend. Great friends are with us wherever we are."

"Why are you so smart?" Jack looked at me raising his hands in surrender. "You're right, I know it. You call out my b.s. That doesn't mean I'll do what you say of course!"

"Of course! Honestly, it's just practice mostly. You ever spend time, real time, with college students? I might be teaching philosophy but mostly my job is to identify and cut through their b.s. meter. If I'm successful, they might have a fighting chance to be a great person later on."

"Kind of an ego trip, isn't that?" Jack was attempting to challenge me this time.

"Yep, completely an ego trip. I think a teacher is as important as any person in their lives at that moment. They hang around peers but mostly their friends are the same way. And if they aren't living at home or if their parents can't do what needs to be done, then it's a teacher–me–who's in a position to have influence. Am I right or successful or effective? When I can be. It doesn't work for some, never will. My words aren't right, or they aren't ready. My point is that I want to try. It's why I teach. Philosophy is my way into the conversation, but it could just as easily be science or sociology... or cooking." "Aren't you Mother Teresa!" "Probably!" I laughed. "Look, I know it sounds profound and weighty, but that's my purpose, my joy. It's why I teach. It's why I'm leaving Ohio. It's why I want to try it somewhere else."

"I love it. Keep it up. Maybe some of it can rub off on me."

We entered Alva and I directed Jack to a regal building on campus, the only one of its kind amongst the mid-century brutalist architecture. We agreed on a time and place for him to pick me, sometime around noon. Is it strange that I almost gave him a kiss on the cheek as he left? Probably. But the idea crossed my mind.

24

JACK

I had time to kill so I first wandered about campus. I poked my head into the bookstore and thumbed through the shirts and sweatshirts and actually bought a faded T-shirt with the college acronym across the front. It would look good in New York, an inside joke for me and Derek. Elitist New Yorkers would think it fashionable and trendy and wonder what boutique could supply such an offbeat item. They would wonder what the acronym would mean, maybe an African term I would need to explain, all the while laughing on the inside that the thing cost $8.99 and it was really just crappy college fodder. God, New York is the worst.

I wandered into the library, read the local newspaper, asked if they had a copy of the New York Times–they didn't–then found my way to the town square which abutted the campus. Like Kiowa, there were the common stores–the antique place, the women's clothing store, the Dollar General, two insurance agencies, a diner serving breakfast and lunch only, as well as a couple of empty storefronts. I began to see possibilities. The conversation with Beth had affected me, perhaps, deeper than conversations with anyone else, other than Derek. She was really challenging me to bring out what I wanted in this life. It wasn't New York. It wasn't my job cooking basic comfort fare. The job I once had was just that, a job. Maybe all I was good at was talking a big game but never getting on the field.

My reverie was broken by an older woman walking by with Dollar General bags in her hands. She stopped and asked what I was looking at.

"Possibilities maybe. Just looking at these storefronts and wondering what they could be."

"Would be great if something new could go in. We got a good town, but things are leaving and the college kids need a place just like the community does. Wish I was younger. I might take a stab at a dress shop or my husband is a pretty good small engine repair man. But that's probably not what the new kids want, is it?"

She smiled at me in that knowing way of an experienced generation. If this were New York, the conversation would have ended sooner or really wouldn't ever have started at all. In my mind, I could see the New York version of this going something like, "What the f are you talking to me for? Nothing to see here. Move on!" But it's Oklahoma. We kept talking.

"What used to be here?"

"It was a dinner place. Served homecooked meals. Was packed just about every night. Even the college kids came."

"What happened?"

"The owner died in a car accident out near Capron. Decided to go over the train tracks when the gates were down. Late for something or other, I guess. The train kept coming and well, you know."

"No one wanted to take it over?"

"Nope, it was here one day, gone the next. Been empty now for a couple of years."

"Interesting …" I let my voice fade.

"Well, you have a good day. You better get going. Storm is coming up pretty good. Saw on the radar some bad stuff out in the Panhandle."

I looked up at the sky as the woman wandered off. In my time staring at empty storefronts and conversing with wise old women, the sky had turned from a musty blue, a bit overcast, to something darker and more ominous. The clouds were streaked with an angry gray, some billowing, others more jagged. The wind had started to pick up–and then there was a stillness. I could smell the rain before it came.

But I also knew the sights and sounds of a bad storm coming, maybe a tornado. It was instinct, something you know just by living on the Plains during the summer. I had never actually seen a tornado, only pictures of other parts of Oklahoma damaged by it. But I had sat outside on the back porch of the farm and watched as storms came in from the west. It was the same. A leaden sky, fierce winds, then stillness.

There were a few times as a kid when all of us, Mom and Jill and me, had headed to the basement. When the storms came up, Mom always had a radio at hand. There aren't tornado sirens out by the farm so the only way you knew to take shelter was to listen to disembodied voices saying that Adams County residents were under a tornado warning–the worst of all–and needed to take cover immediately.

That's when we went to the basement, down through the washroom off the kitchen to what looked like an innocuous closet but housed a set of stairs down to a dark one-room shelter with a single dangling light bulb. We shared space with the canning supplies and the innumerable jars of pickles and tomatoes and okra and beans. There is another entry way to the shelter from the outside, a slanted door into the ground, always padlocked for some unknown reason. I never knew why, just that it had always been that way.

We would sometimes hear the thunder up above, a low rumble from the shelter underground, and we would wait things out until the radio said the warning was over. I always went out to inspect the farm after those times. I was sure the world had changed, and I wanted to be the first to see it in its newness. Inevitably there were branches strewn about and puddles from the heavy rain but one time there was a tree that had cracked across the top of the trunk, the heavy branches toppled over, the tree bowing to its companions who had not succumbed to the weather. Another time there was a door ripped off the barn. I found it in one of the fields. I don't remember who fixed it but I wondered if tornadoes could fly me far away from Oklahoma. It was my Wizard of Oz thing.

I went to the car and found the local station.

> *A tornado watch has been issued for Adams County in Oklahoma and Hall County in Kansas and the local communities of Alva, Capron, and Kiowa. Again, a tornado watch has been issued for Adams County and Hall County. Residents are advised that severe weather is likely to occur and that conditions are positive for a tornado to occur. Taking shelter in your home is advised and caution should be maintained if outside.*

I made two quick calls. Beth's phone immediately went to voicemail. "Beth, it's Jack. Didn't know if you were done there yet. Instead of meeting at the car, why don't I come your way and we can wait out the storm in one of the university buildings.

I'll meet you in the lobby. I'm on my way now. Need to give Jill a call. Bye."

The second call was picked up immediately.

"Jill, honey, you ok?" I was trying to keep my voice neutral. I didn't want to scare her with my own anxiety.

"I'm fine. How are you?"

"Good, I mean, I'm about to get Beth. But it says the weather is getting bad. Have you looked outside?"

I could hear her moving over to a window and lifting up the shades wherever she was in the house.

"It looks real dark. The trees are going crazy in the shelter-belt."

"Jill, honey." I stopped and wondered why I called her Jill-honey in times of stress. It's a habit. A way to calm her down. A way to calm me down.

"Jill, I think a storm is coming your way. I was listening to the radio, and it said a tornado watch was activated. Can you turn on the TV and see what's happening?"

"I'll do it right now."

There was a silence while Jill shuffled over to the TV. Then I could hear the weatherman talking and imagined him as a middle-aged native Oklahoman, plain but inviting in that weatherman sort of way.

"We've got a cell here just west of Capron. Looks like it will be hitting just north of there in about ten minutes. No tornado reported yet but heavy winds and golf-ball sized hail. Winds have been reported up to fifty miles per hour. If you are in that vicinity, stay inside."

"Jill? Jill?" I waited until she seemed to track back to my voice.

"Yes, what?"

"Did you hear that? A big storm. Stay inside and away from the windows, OK?"

"Silly, I always stay inside!" I had to laugh.

"Sorry, yes, I know you stay inside. But stay away from the windows. What happens if a tornado comes?"
"I know to go to the basement. But ..." "What Jill?"

"Well, I don't think I can get there anymore. Some things fell down last year and then Mom moved an old refrigerator out of the way and put it by the entrance. It's really heavy."

"Wait, what? Why?"
"Because she died!" Jill practically screamed at me. "I'm sorry, I'm sorry." I needed to bring Jill back down.

"Jill, honey, I shouldn't have said that. I know Mom was going to move it. I'm just worried about you, that's all."
In the background I could still hear the weatherman.

"An update. A tornado warning has been issued for the northern part of Adams County, from Capron to the state line. Repeat: A tornado warning has been issued for this section of Adams County."

I imagined him pointing at what was almost directly the farm and where Jill was located at that very moment.

"A tornado warning means that a tornado has been sighted and that people should take cover immediately in a basement or in the interior of the house. Please seek shelter immediately."

Then there was no more weatherman's voice. "Jill, what happened?"

"I think the power went out. The TV just went off and so did the lights."

"Jill, honey, I need you to get to the basement. Do you think you could just walk around the house to the outside cellar door, maybe just this one time? Is it still locked there?"

"NOOOOOOOOOOOO…."

Her voice was a howl, pain and hurt and fear at the deepest levels. "Jill, listen to me. You can take a few steps, right?"

She didn't say anything. Jack knew he was on the verge of losing her. "Jill, ok, then I need you to take cover, the bath or under a bed, or under the table in the kitchen. Go, now."

And then the line cut off. At first, I thought it was Jill hanging up but instinct said otherwise. It was the phone lines being cut by the storm. There was no way to communicate with Jill.

25

JILL

"Jack? Jack, are you there?" I only heard the click and Jack's voice wasn't there anymore. It was kind of like one of those scary shows where someone is talking on the phone but then the lines go silent cause the killer cut 'em all. Those scenes are so predictable I swear cause the killer will creep up in the dark. And if it's the hero then the hero will escape or maybe kill the bad guy but if it's some rube then they're gonna get it. I watched the one called Halloween on Christmas and that's what happened over and over.

So Jack wasn't there anymore. And it was getting really loud outside, not like close to me but like loud from further away. I went over to see out the kitchen windows over by the sink and everything out there was blowing real hard. There were leaves and stuff and dust from the driveway and I couldn't even see that far.

And then the electricity went out.

It made everything seem louder and the light outside was this really cool shimmering light, not really day and not really night but something so cool in between. It was supposed to be the middle of the day! Go explain that to Bill Nye the Science Guy -- by the way, I love that show.

But then it got real still outside. Not quiet, but still. It was loud as all get-out, but it was from over there by the shelter belt and it even seemed to be getting closer and closer. I could tell it was coming my way, sort of like over by Ray's place but closer than that. I looked over at those trees and suddenly one of them flipped in the air. Then another. Then another. I was like matches getting tossed up in the air, I tell you. I did that trick once and called it "Fifty-two Pickup" like the card game. Mom didn't think that one was funny at all, but I did.

And then the house started to shake. I didn't know where that was coming from at all. But it was like the whole house was shaking. And me with it. This was maybe getting a little scary. Jack had mentioned a tornado so maybe now was the time to get protected.

I had read once that the place from a tornado was some room on the inside of the house, like away from windows, maybe a closet or bathroom. But every closet in our house was filled with stuff, well, mostly my stuff cause Mom would give me what I wanted like new stainless-steel bowls or a hand-held blender or such. I had like three blenders in total in those very closets because I needed the best one. Go with the expensive one I tell you. So no closets to go to and definitely not the bathroom cause it was really close to the back yard and truthfully I'd just taken a number two in there so it was kind of stinky.
So where could I go?

To the kitchen, I tell you! It was also kind of inside of the whole house, especially the dining room side of things. If I laid like under the table and put all the chairs around me I would be super protected. I did forts like that in the living room, so I knew for sure it would work in the kitchen.

I ran super-fast and grabbed two blankets off my bed and a couple of pillows and got back to the kitchen in no time. The house was really starting to shake then. I draped the blankets really careful over the table and made sure they would stay put by putting parts of the blanket under the chair legs and wrapping it around. I know my forts, I tell you. It didn't take me any time at all 'cause I am like a super fort making expert.

I crawled in my fort and put my pillows down on the floor. Seeing how I didn't have my cookbooks or magazines to read, which is what I normally do in my forts, I put my head down curled into my sleeping ball. I have to be in a ball to sleep. I just have to. I've tried stretching out, on my tummy, all of 'em. But no way, Jose. A sleeping ball it is. Real cozy, you know.

And I said my prayers because, well, it just seemed like the right thing to do.

> *Now I lay me down to sleep,*
> *I pray the lord my soul to keep.*
> *If I should die before I wake,*
> *I pray the Lord my soul to take.*
> *Amen.*
> *Bless Jack and Beth and Ray and my mom in heaven.*

Then I went to sleep.

26

BETH

The farmhouse was obliterated. There were no standing walls. Instead, only a pile of materials that might have once been a house. I'd only seen destruction like that from a wrecking ball. Piles of rubble everywhere, trees torn from their foundations. Jack was frantically moving from place to place searching for her until we located what looked like where the interior of the house should have been.

We both ran that way calling out Jill's name but heard no response. We pulled back the wreckage desperately hoping to find her. There was the front door, there, the sink from the bathroom. Both next to each other in a place that didn't seem to be anywhere near their original home.

"Where would she go?" There was fear in my voice.

"Nowhere. That's the problem."

Jack made his way into what would have been the kitchen. Appliances were turned over and the stove was gone. But there was the kitchen table, that solid piece of oak we had sat at days before. And under the kitchen table was the hint of clothing, a dress maybe, peering out. We ran over to it, Jack moving quicker and tossing pieces of house here and there to get to her. He cleared away debris and pushed away the table. It was Jill.

She looked asleep. Not damaged or injured, just asleep. The table had clearly protected her, kept her cocooned. While other things had flown about, she stayed out of harm's way. But maybe there was damage we couldn't see.

"Jill?" Jack yelled down at her wishing desperately for a response. None came.

"Beth, does she look ok to you?"

"Nothing wrong I can see. She's breathing right?" Jack leaned down and nodded.

"She is. But what do we do? We have to get her out of here. What then? She can't be outside. And what if she's hurt? We're not supposed to move a hurt person even when they're unconscious!" Jack was still frantic, three steps ahead and worried what would happen when Jill came to.

"Jack, stop for a moment." I was trying to keep cool. "She seems fine but right now we need to get her out of this place. You're right. She can't wake up here so let's move her to Ray's place. Somehow his house escaped all this."

Jack moved Jill carefully, extracting her from the chaos of the destroyed house. He picked her up and cradled her in his arms, just like a small child and laid her carefully in the back of the car. She didn't stir as we drove the quarter mile to Ray's.

Ray was getting in his truck as we drove up. He ran over to us. "I was just coming over to check on Jill. I was in the basement until we got the all-clear. You all OK?" He turned and saw Jill. I don't think he realized we had already been over to the other place.

"Oh my God. Is Jill Ok? Is she hurt?"

I reached out to Ray and put my hand on his shoulder. "We

think so. But we should probably get Jill inside. Jack?"

I looked over at Jack and he was already in the midst of carrying Jill inside. We put Jill into the spare bedroom on the main floor next to my room. She still didn't stir even when we got her wet clothes off and into a nightgown that didn't quite fit. Jack seemed sheepish at seeing his sister's nakedness as a grown woman. I reached out to him.

"It's ok. You're taking care of her, like a father. Nothing to be ashamed of and nothing to shy away from. Don't be such a tough guy!" I was hoping to shed some of the tension in the room. His shoulders relaxed.

We left her to sleep and went to call the doctor. The lines were still dead, both the traditional landlines from Ray's phone and my cell phone. It was a constant busy signal.

Ray spoke up then. "Just let her be. We can't get anyone on the line, and she seems comfortable. Maybe it's just her body doing the work it needs to do to heal and get rid of the stress. She's protecting herself."

Jack stopped for a moment and looked up at Ray. But it seemed to hit him then, the magnitude of it all. The house he had known for a lifetime, even with all his anger, that house that formed him, was gone. He looked empty, not that he didn't know how to answer Ray, but that there was nothing inside to answer with. The house would need to be rebuilt. Maybe Jack as well.

But Jill was here and safe. Jack went over to the chair in the corner of the room. I slipped out a few minutes later, Jack seeming not to notice. When I came back in, his eyes were closed, fast asleep like his sister.

27

JACK

It was sundown when I started to stir. The last rays of light came filtering into the room. I could see Jill sitting up in the bed. It startled me.

"Jill, you awake?"

"I am. Why am I in this bed?"

She said it matter-of-factly, vintage Jill. Her question borne out of curiosity rather than anxiety. It was like she knew she was supposed to be waking up somewhere in her house, that the tradition of her own bed and her own place was fixed, but now she was somewhere else, and it didn't make sense.

"Are you ok? Are you feeling ok?"

"Yes, Silly. I'm fine." Same tone, same Jill. "But where am I? I don't know this place. I mean, you're here, but I don't know it." She paused. "Is there anything to eat?"

I smiled and wondered if Jill could see it. "Do you remember anything at all?"

"Well, you called and then the phone went out. And I remember there being big sounds outside so I made a fort under the kitchen table. I couldn't go in the bathroom, there was already a hole in the ceiling when I went there."

I stared at her. She talked so casually about a tornado taking away parts of the house and her building a fort to protect herself. "But weren't you scared?"

"Well, yeah, duh. But the kitchen seemed safe and fine and there weren't any problems even with all the terrible sounds. I just put my head down and kind of fell asleep."

"You slept?"

"Yeah, it was cool. I fell asleep really fast. I remember this one show I watched once where this girl was in terrible danger and she fell asleep and it helped her hide because she was really quiet. I guess she didn't snore!" Jill snorted in laughter. "The doctor on the show said it was because she was protecting herself, that the body was a beautiful thing and always could sense danger. Do you think that happened to me?"

Whether it was sleep as a defense or being knocked unconscious, my sister had missed the tornado altogether.

"Maybe so, honey, maybe so."

"So where am I?"

"You are at Ray's place. Do you ever remember being here?"

"Whoa, cool!" Jill seemed seriously delighted at the thought of being at Ray's. I didn't get it. I didn't get her.

"Doesn't that bother you, like, that you had to go outside to get here?"

"Not really." She said it without hesitation. "I mean, I went outside, but I don't remember it. I didn't see it. I didn't experience it. So for all I know, I've always been inside. And this is cool. I get to see another place!"

"Is Beth here? Ray?"

"They are but ..."

"But what?"

"The farm is destroyed. It's gone. The house is gone. The tornado wiped it out. We pulled you from the wreckage."

"Really? That is so cool. I mean, not cool that the house is gone, but that I am the survivor! Can we call the news and have them come interview me?"

It was fully dark now. I couldn't see her across the room, but I could see her smile and her child-like joy. I remembered Mom's letter. Jill was truly okay as long as she was somewhere safe inside. It didn't matter where. "Home" for her could be just about anywhere.

"Do you think you could stay here for a while?"

"Well, of course, silly. I mean, where else are we going to go?" What a great answer. The perfect answer.

I wandered into the living room not really knowing what to do next. The phone didn't work, so there was not a doctor or insurance person to call right now. I couldn't go look for my clothes or minor possessions I had brought with me because it was dark and no electricity in sight. It was a stalemate, me against the world right now. The world couldn't do much with me and I couldn't do much with it.

"Just sit, will you?" Beth had noticed me standing still. "Sit and breathe for a minute. You're alive, she's alive. The storm's passed. But you've got to sit and collect. You can move forward tomorrow."

"That sounds like some philosophical bullshit you read somewhere." I grinned at her, so she knew I was kidding. But I was also scared, and I didn't want her to see that fear. She saw it.

"No, not philosophy. If it were that, I'd be asking you about your essential nature right now and the whims of the unfeeling life. Nope, it's just me. You look ..." She paused like she always does. "You look lost and maybe hurt and a little bewildered. Ray always said when that happens we need to stop and pause and look for our blessings. It's a little country, but Ray the Shaman is pretty good."

I sat down. I laid my head down on the sofa cushions, finding peace in their soft embrace.

"Mind if I come over there with you?"

She came to sit down next to me and pulled my head into her lap. It felt good to be cared for. But then she put one arm on my chest and bent over to kiss me. It was the first one. Soft and caring, not hesitant, not fast.

I pulled away and asked. "Why the kiss? I thought that was supposed to be me at some point in the near future."

"Because I wanted to and you needed it and so did I." I pulled her down for another, this one much longer. "You're right. I did need that."

I laid there with her for a long time, closing my eyes, and enjoying the silence. I didn't need to ask any more questions. The answers would come later.

Apres-Diner Sweet

BETH

It's actually been great to have Jack and Jill here in the house. I bet some would think of it as an intrusion but there's something to having people around. I haven't lived with somebody, anybody, for a decade. I haven't had a roommate at all since my second year of college. I mean, there was the one guy who just stayed with me - "shacked up" in graduate school - but he still had his own apartment and his own closet.

Jill has been a whirl. The doctor did come to check her out and other than a scratch on her leg from flying debris and a small bump on her head, she was fine. He thinks the bump is what knocked her out, or at least made her woozy. He also thinks her body just shut down, a kind of self-induced coma, to protect her from the anxiety of the storm and the house being ripped apart. I've asked Jill a couple of times what she remembers. Mostly she says nothing and smiles, but one time she paused for a second and her face got real serious. It was as if some memory was trying to break through, that it was intruding on her defenses, but as quickly as it came, it disappeared. I'm not going to push it. She's happy here and now. Why mess that up?

Ray might be the happiest of all. I don't think I understood how lonely he was.

Frankly, he might not have understood the same thing until we all came to live with him. He spends a lot of his time in the kitchen with Jill. Sometimes he'll join her at the stove or on a chopping board, but mostly he just sits and talks to her. When I've overheard them, the talk has been about food, about old TV shows, about what Ray can get out of the garden, what they will can and put up for the winter, old music versus new music.

It's an endless stream. For Jill, it's someone who listens. For Ray–well, for Ray I think it's like being a parent again and having someone to care for. My cheap psychology tells me he's dying and he doesn't want to be taken care of. It's his Midwestern rural stiff upper lip. He'd rather take care of someone else. We all let him. I'm grateful for being here and spending the last months of his life together.

I did get the job at the college. I teach two classes every day. It's hard and busy and when you figure a per hour pay basis I'm basically making less than someone at McDonald's. And I love it. These are different students than the ones I previously had. Most are farm kids from the area, some are athletes brought from here and there - mostly urban areas - to play a sport and maybe get an education. Many don't care.

They especially don't care about literature and philosophy and religion or anything to do with what I teach. But I reach them. I know I reach them. We don't talk as much about the books as we do about big ideas and big questions, the things that might just pertain to their lives. How to be a good person, what's our purpose, how do we care for one another. Even farm kids and athletes want those answers.

And Jack? That's been a whirlwind. The first kiss turned into a few more kisses, some stolen in quick moments, a few more on a date. One day Ray turned to me and said, "You guys ever gonna make this formal?" I blushed. I rarely blush. Jill chimed in with her two cents. "Come on, you need to get a room!" She was quite proud of herself with that snappy contribution. I laughed and asked how they knew. Ray said it was obvious and almost out of a bad Hallmark movie. Jill cackled at that. It was in the glances, the eyes, the hand touches that he noticed. He was right. Jack and I were getting closer.

But the issue was two-fold. He still had an unease about him. Unsettled Jack was not the best version of himself. When I asked, he said he just didn't know what to do with himself. He wanted to cook regularly but he wasn't. He wanted the bustle of the city, but really treasured the silences he was finding here. He was used to the distance between him and Jill but now she was right there.

The other issue was right in front of him. "And what about me? Do I make you uneasy?" He immediately said yes. He had been with girls but he proclaimed me a woman. I think what he really meant was that I was more mature and that he was more serious. I haven't asked him the dreaded future question - where are we headed? - but I can see that it's coming. We've taken steps. He doesn't sleep in the basement room anymore. When it became clear to everyone that we were "together" it seemed natural for him to move upstairs to my room. I'll give him credit though. He was the one to ask if this was ok. Small steps for Jack. He's softening.

I think we're both waiting for some kind of resolution. We're on autopilot right now. Not that it's bad because the release from tension - my move, the tornado, Jack's job loss and move from NYC, Ray's illness - is healthy. We all just need to breathe and it's nice to be able to do it together. But we'll have to get off autopilot at some point and land the plane. What happens when Ray passes away? Does Jack go back to NYC? If so, what does that mean for us? For Jill?

Jack has started the process of rebuilding the farmhouse. His mom kept up on the insurance and had a decent rider for tornado issues. Cost a lot, Jack found out later, but somehow his mom knew this might be important someday, for her and for Jill. I don't think she ever assumed Jack would be part of that equation. The homebuilder met with Jack last week to talk about designs. When I asked him about it he pushed me off, said it wasn't quite right and that he needed to think on things. He would be getting back with the homebuilder the next month. He said the homebuilder wanted to do an almost exact replica of what had been there previously, an homage to his mom and frankly the easiest and simplest thing to do. Jack said he might need something new, that somehow he needed to make it his own or Jill's own or just something else. He couldn't quite articulate it and I knew to just let him have the space to figure it out.

Harvest has come and gone and the winter wheat has been planted. There's not much but brown in the fields but a golden glow fills the landscape with autumnal light. I love that. I never realized how much I love it. I haven't been back at this time of year for a while and I understand now what I was missing.

My favorite time of night is dusk. Sometimes Jack and I will take a walk down to where his mom's place was. It's a short walk, a quarter mile like every section around here. It's cool then and as we walk east the sun is setting behind us. The purples and pinks of a Midwest sky play off the landscape. We'll walk out in the field too. Inevitably Jack will pick some leftover stalk that didn't make it through harvest, rub off the skins and hand me a wheat kernel. It's still a little chewy and earthy and magical. He'll smile. I'll do the same. We'll hold hands and keep walking until the sun goes down. It's nice.

JILL

I totally love living with Ray and Beth and Jack. It is so much fun! Ray cooks with me all the time or at least he talks to me while I cook. Mom wouldn't do that as much.

She kept to herself mostly, especially the last couple of years. But Ray is so cool. The other day he brought me some okra and some zucchini and some peppers from his garden. I didn't know what to do with it right away, so he showed me how to make fried okra and then we pickled some. And the squash and peppers was a side dish with some herbs he got there also. It was an Italian dish I learned from Giada. I showed Ray how to do that one and he was totally excited about it.

I know he's dying. But he told me not to be sad so I'm not. I like this way a lot better than my mom. If my mom could have told me then maybe I could have prepared for it better, but she didn't. I'm still sad she's gone but I don't think about it as much. I think Ray and me are going to have a great time until he dies. He told me there will be a time when he will just be tired and have to be in bed most days. I told him that I would serve him every meal in bed and be his nurse! How cool is that?

And I totally love my room here! It's bigger than what I used to have. Beth helped me set up a library of cookbooks. In my own room even! She even goes to the library in Alva and gets me some new ones to look at. Mom never really did that. I mean she went to the Kiowa library now and then but with Beth it's every single week. She got me one on Greek cooking the other day. It's the best! I want to make moussaka now and maybe some stuffed grape leaves but I don't know where to get those. Maybe on Amazon? Like everything is on Amazon but I don't have an account now since Mom died. I don't think I should ask Jack about that yet.

I asked Beth about teaching, and she says she really loves it. I asked her if she would teach me too since I couldn't ever go to college. Beth was real quiet for a second and I thought maybe I had said something wrong so I told her I was kidding and kind of laughed it off. But Beth looked at me real serious and said if I was really serious too then she would love to teach me. She would have me be a student in one of her classes, well not really a student, but she would teach me on my own just like those students and make me do the assignments and everything. She said we could maybe even have me enroll in an online class after that. OMG, I might go to college!!

But what would I study? I mean I love cooking but I kind of like stories and making things up. Beth told me to start with her class and all the stories she teaches. Her favorite one is this one called "Bartleby the Scrivener". I know because I read it the next day. You can find, like, any old story or book online and I read the whole thing. It was weird. It was about this guy who kept saying he preferred not to do anything at all but the guy who was his boss kept asking and then didn't know what to do. No way Jose! He should have fired his butt quick! Like on Shark

Tank or Undercover Boss. That's how they do it there.

The other thing that Beth did was start to help me with my hair. I know, I know, it's just hair and I didn't really care. Mom always cut it herself like every two weeks. She just cut the front bangs and then trimmed some off the sides and kind of kept it the same. But Beth said I should just grow it out. Cool! I didn't know I could and that is like the best cause I want my hair to look like those people in the magazines. They have pretty hair and my old hair made me pretty much look like a stupid boy … which is really stupid! Beth said she has a friend who cuts hair and she can come out to our house to cut mine. OMG, again how cool! Beth is like this sister I never had. She helped me pick out some new clothes on Amazon cause the tornado made all my other ones fly away. I even got a dress and wore it at dinner last week. I never had a dress! Well, I mean I had a dress, but it was from when I was fifteen and I kind of got bigger since then, like all over. Even my butt! Beth is totally the best!

And the bestest thing ever, even better than my dress? Jack and Beth are kissing!!! I saw it one time when they were trying to sneak but I caught them and then me and Ray told them to get a room! They did! Jack moved his stuff into Beth's room and now they're together. I hope they get married and have kids and things. I told them that too and both of them told me to slow down. Slow down??? Come on people, get with the program. If you totally love someone like they do, then get married and have kids. That's what happens on the Hallmark movies. And it should happen with them!

Jack's nice and better to me now. We even laugh together and cook together sometimes. Last week he asked if I might make a pie and even make an appetizer. He was going to try something called a "pop up" which is when you suddenly have a restaurant for a day and invite people you might know but don't really know. He said he advertised at the college with the teachers there and he had ten people say 'yes' like, right away.

He set up tables with nice tablecloths next to the garden under the big tree. I could see from the window what he was doing. And we totally cooked together. I made two really cool appetizers with okra. I know, okra! After Ray had taught me then I kept cooking with it because it is like a weed you know. Ray brings tons and tons of it from his garden each day. I made one that was called Southern Sushi which has pickled okra - I did that the day before! - with cream cheese and really good prosciutto and then I grilled okra and grilled jalapeños together. OMG, the best! Jack told me people love it. Jack did something called farm-to-table which was to make everything from the garden except for some pork he bought. He had two or three salads and some grilled veg and some really cool herbs on the chicken. And then everyone ate my peach pie with Jack's homemade lavender ice cream. It was a hit! And Jack was so happy.

I asked him yesterday about the other house. He says he's just not sure. He's got an "idea brewing" ... what the heck does that mean anyway? He says he wants to rebuild it, but I'm not going there for sure and who would live there? He joked and said maybe we need to knock me out again and while I'm out they take me over to the new house and then I live there forever. I don't think I want to. I mean, they could knock me out, I guess. It worked in the tornado and I'm fine now. But I just don't think I want to be there anymore. I like it here. This is my home now.

JACK

I think I've figured out where I belong. Weird thing, it's here. Let me rephrase that. It's not weird and home is where I can finally feel at ease. I don't need to fight any more like I used to in New York City. Fight for space, fight for voice, fight for my place. Hell, I don't even swear that much anymore. Only when I'm really mad - which just isn't that often - or I cut my finger chopping something. Funny how life changes when you have space and you have voice and you have … someone.

It's been four months since the tornado. And maybe one of the worst days of my life has actually given me the opportunity to be better, a lot better. The rebuild won't be done for another six months and that's ok. I'm comfortable here. We all seem to be comfortable here at Ray's place. A while back I might have thought it would be awful, living with Jill, living in Oklahoma at all. But it's nice to have a place to come back to each day and happy faces to greet us. I know, I know, I sound like a f .., I sound like a rube. But I love to see Jill happy and Ray makes her happy. He gets to be dad and I get to be big brother.

I called Derek the other day and told him I wouldn't be back.

Ever. I told him he could take my shi…, my stuff, and keep it or sell it or whatever. I only asked him to send my chef's knives and my records. Even the clothes aren't worth it. I don't miss anything. Derek said he knew about two months ago I wasn't coming back but he waited me out to say it. He's already got a new roommate, also a cross dresser, but he says they don't compete. He's more glam and Nancy Sinatra while Derek still maintains his elegant style with heels and pearls. I told him to come visit me. He said maybe. He said he needs to meet this Beth girl who seems to have stolen my heart.

She has. Stolen my heart most completely. I don't understand it like so much else here and when I ask her she just shrugs her shoulders and says why does it have to be any way at all. There's no time limit or rules or anything for falling in love, she says. She's right, I know it, but it seems strange to fall in love with someone in a week and stay in love with them for four months. And then ask them to move in with you at a house that's being built next door to the one that's supposed to be yours. It's weird she said yes.

So the plan is to have Jill stay here, to be with Ray until he passes on. Then the house is hers, her place, the box she will live in. When Beth finally confronted me and said to stop taking care of her, just to let her live and be, it finally made sense. I don't need to babysit her. She's quite capable of being on her own. It's not about whether she can go outside or has to stay inside or has anxiety over things. Nope, it's about her being independent and being ok. We can pay some bills, check on her and get her ingredients and do those things, but she is perfectly fine. The problem was never her. It was always me.

I think a lot of the change has been Jill having a purpose. Her place was always inside, but Mom never gave her purpose. For

Mom, her own purpose was taking care of Jill but never giving over anything to her. Jill's got two things right now. She's just finishing up Beth's course, but she's already officially enrolled in two online courses next semester. She feels powerful because of that, and I can almost see her growing. The other night at the table she started talking about The Iliad and why Achilles was so sad and so angry. She wondered what it would be like to lose a friend like he did.

Her other purpose is food. She's a cook, and come to find out, she's a damn good one. I guess when you have time on your hands and not a lot of other distractions you can get good quickly. She and Ray have been spending a lot of time in the kitchen. He gave her a bunch of garden things and then she started pickling and canning and preserving. A couple of nights each week she makes dinner and I'll be damned if it isn't restaurant quality. And I tell her so.

Late in the summer I asked her to help out with an idea I had, a pop-up restaurant, like the ones starting to get big in the City. I had wanted to try it but really didn't have the courage. Beth gave me the courage, so I did it. I asked around at the college to see if there might be interest and then even did a quick bulletin board announcement in the building where Beth's office is. Bam! Just like that, I had a full table, ten people who wanted to be at my place on the farm, eating my food. And they all showed up.

I asked Jill to do the appetizer and the dessert. It was killer. Better than my main entree of roast Szechuan pork — local, of course--with quick-fire garden vegetables. She nailed it. People asked when the next one was and I panicked and said in two weeks. Two weeks later, twelve people showed up because the original ten brought two friends. I had to pull extra chairs out of the house, like comfortable chairs, rather than the folding ones.

It actually added to the ambience.

Again, Jill was killer. I did a spicy garden pasta for the entree – homemade noodles and all – while Jill did an appetizer of pork dumplings and collard greens and a fresh strawberry tart with basil. At the end of the night, we had scheduled the next two months. I had no idea what the hell I was doing, but people seemed to want it and were willing to pay for it. Finally, Beth asked what we do when the weather got bad. After some rumbling on it and more conversation, a business plan started to form. I would do a pop-up every week from mid-May to basically October 15. The other part of the year – I would do it inside at the diner I had seen in Alva on the square. A pop-up on Thursday, Friday, and Saturday only when the college kids are around. Summer months I stay on the farm.

I've had the talks already about renting the space in Alva and modifying it. It doesn't need much. The equipment is still good, and the decor is solid. I don't need fancy or a theme. I just need people to come for a decent meal. If the current pop-ups are any indication, then this will work out. I'm not going to be rich, but I'll be happy. My sister will be happy because she'll make all the appetizers and desserts and maybe an entree now and then for the pop-ups. I already told her she needs to make all the desserts for the restaurant. She's stoked beyond belief. She has purpose.

All of this … well, it's part of the design of the new farmhouse where Beth and I will live. It will be our home and maybe we've talked about having a bedroom or two for kids, but I don't think we're serious yet. She's waiting for me to put a ring on her finger and if I tell you the truth, I bought something yesterday. I don't know the moment when I'll ask but it's coming soon. She better the hell say yes.

But the house. The kitchen will be its literal and figurative heart. Lots of places for family to gather there. I know Jill won't be there, but we'll make a special seat just for her that no one can ever sit in because her spirit will always be there. I want to keep the door that comes from the dirt driveway into the kitchen but out front where the porch sits I'll be putting in a patio. It will look down to the creek and the trees, away from the sun as it sets. It's the perfect place to do pop-ups. I've already got designs for an outdoor fire pit and a brick oven for some special kinds of gatherings and meals.

That's my place, the place maybe I'll stay forever. I'm more settled now and don't really feel a pull to move on. I could, but I don't want to. It's no longer the inertia of some small job in some small restaurant in some big city with no real future and no real options. No, it's me wanting this here to be my place. Maybe that's the point. Jill never really had a choice. She always had to stay in one place, and she made it her home. But It's not her prison. It's her gift, I think. I've learned - heck, maybe Jill taught me - that home isn't about geography even though that's how we talk about it. My home is there, my place is there, that's my land. No, home is what we create. Home is with people and with ourselves and perhaps tied to a place. Home for me is here, now, in Oklahoma.

What would Mom think of that?

Acknowledgments

Writing is often a solitary endeavor but a finished novel is rarely the product of being alone. My many thanks go out to Roxie Kirk, an editor of the first degree who made this work better … and better … and then better still. To my parents, Randy and Barbara, who read initial drafts and suggested that maybe there was something here. We need that initial support when we bring to light what has been in the dark for so long. Finally, this story and this novel does not come to being without my wife Carol. She read, she encouraged, but her influence is much deeper and much more profound. She has wandered with me across the country over our thirty years together inhabiting home after home after home, always making the next as beautiful as the last. May we all find a welcoming home to return to as I have found each day with her.

Travis Feezell *has served in a variety of positions in higher education for over three decades including baseball coach, professor, and college president. With degrees ranging from British Medieval Studies to Sport in American Higher Education, he has written widely on a variety of non-fiction topics over that time. This is his first novel but certainly not his first attempt to come to terms with his love for food and drink and the beauty of family and home. He currently resides in Charlotte, North Carolina with Carol, his wife of thirty years, and Kevin, his cat of five years.*